The Nobodies

ONLY VILLAINS CAN SAVE THIS PLANET

ALEKSANDAR MILJKOVIC

◆ FriesenPress

Suite 300 - 990 Fort St
Victoria, BC, V8V 3K2
Canada

www.friesenpress.com

ISBN
978-1-5255-8130-4 (Hardcover)
978-1-5255-8131-1 (Paperback)
978-1-5255-8132-8 (eBook)

1. FICTION, FANTASY, CONTEMPORARY

Distributed to the trade by The Ingram Book Company

TABLE OF CONTENTS

CHAPTER 1

Victor Volta

Do you want to know about Victor?

Well, ask the old neighbors who have known him since he was a little boy. They will tell you how he was a little angel who never forgot to say "Good morning" and even carried their bags of fruits and vegetables home from the market when they looked too heavy.

Or ask his schoolmates. They will be thrilled to talk about him! How many times did he help them on tests? Not to mention how many girls they met because of him . . . Those bastards.

Why don't you ask his family? Of course, his family will say the best-possible things; that's what family does.

His coworkers will say he's always there for them with a simple thing such as a shift swap and working extra hours when needed just to help them out.

Then there's his beloved wife. On second thought, don't ask her. She can talk about Victor for days, and trust me, not one word will be negative!

Even his dog, the damn thing will bark like a thunder if he feels anyone has bad intentions toward Victor!

Oh well . . .

Wait a second . . . I know!

Try asking the dead man in Victor's trunk. Ask those wide-open eyes, the only eyes who have seen the true Victor.

Try to understand the last whisper that ran out of his mouth full of blood . . .

On second thought, don't ask anything because those cold ears will not hear you. Don't ask. Go away. Far away . . .

And be a good friend to Victor. Or be his family, his wife, coworker, schoolmate . . .

Don't be anybody else because you never know . . .

Maybe tomorrow, he will smile at you in the market and say, "Good morning," and maybe that same night while your soul is leaving your body, he will say, "Goodnight."

Victor has just returned from his job as a manager for one of the city's steakhouses.

"Honey, I'm home!" Through half-open door, a smile on his face, he announces his arrival.

"Dinner's ready!" his wife, Lucy, says, proving again what an amazing wife she is. "Come on up!"

Leonardo, their black, muscular Doberman, jumps on Victor just inside the door.

"Hey, you miss me?" Victor asks. "Or do you smell that I have something for you?" He crouches while hiding something behind his back.

As Leo tries to lick his face, Victor moves his head in circles, giving the dog a taste of his shiny black hair instead. As he stands up, Leo finally manages to kiss him on the lips!

"Next time Leo will prepare dinner for you if he's the one who gets kissed first!" Lucy says, standing in front of them, pretending to be mad with her hands on her hips and her head tilted to the side as if she doesn't want to see him.

"Did I tell you how beautiful you look this evening?" Victor asks. With a smile on the edge of his lips and his left eyebrow arched, he moves closer to her while dropping a snack for Leo behind his back. As they kiss, Leo grabs the snack and runs into another room.

"OK, Mr. Sweet Mouth," Lucy says. "Let's go upstairs before dinner gets cold." She takes his hand and pulls him up the steps.

Their house isn't one of the biggest in the neighborhood, and it's also one of the oldest in Vancouver, but Victor grew up there, and he never wants to leave it. He has "too many memories in there," as he says.

They painted it light blue with white doors and windows and renovated certain parts. They took a lot of time detailing the house—especially Lucy, who is crazy about her garden. Strawberries, raspberries, cherry tomatoes, onions, pretty much anything that can grow from the ground!

As much as Lucy is crazy about her garden, Victor is in love with his garage. He loves to spend time there, working on his car and on his computer. It's a silent, peaceful place.

Lucy is twenty-nine, but she looks much younger, maybe because of her black hair, which almost touches her shoulders. She wears it in a style that kids in primary school normally wear, and the positive energy that she exudes makes her look like a child at certain moments. However, she's extremely mature and smart when it comes to serious situations in life. She keeps a cool head and makes good decisions. Sometimes Victor disagrees with her, but he cannot say no when she comes close to him with those big black eyes. Sometimes he's not sure if she's going to kill him or kiss him.

Lucy is quite jealous, but she's good at hiding that from Victor. He used to get a lot of "Hey, are you Robin?", pointing out that he looks a lot like a Joseph Gordon-Levitt, who played Robin in *The Dark Knight Rises*, the last part of Christopher Nolan's Batman trilogy. That caused her to go ballistic at the beginning of their relationship, but now that they have been married for four years, she's gotten used to it. Sometimes, she even yells "Yes, come take a picture with him!"

By the way, he does look a lot like Joseph Gordon-Levitt! Victor is thirty years old. He has stylish, shiny black hair combed to the right or left, depending on his mood, no beard, small brown eyes, and a charming smile. He and Lucy are a perfect match!

"Thank you, honey, for the delicious meal," he says afterward once they're seated in the living room. "Cherry tomatoes really gave a perfect touch to that salad!"

"They're from my garden!" Lucy says, bouncing on the sofa in the living room as they kiss each other.

He grabs the TV remote off a side table and turns on the TV. "Let's see, what do we have here . . ." he says while surfing from one channel to another.

Lucy puts her head on his shoulder, her eyes half-closed. "How was your day?"

"Not too busy. It's Monday, you know, not exactly the perfect day for the restaurants. But I stayed a bit longer to finish a few things that I've meant to get to since last week."

"M-hmm . . .," Lucy says as her eyes close completely, already falling asleep. Victor always claims she held the world record for falling asleep the quickest!

Victor turns the TV up slightly, so he can hear the young red-headed TV host, careful not to wake Lucy up.

"His family claims Mr. Wilson always calls them if he knows he'll be home later than expected. They're scared that something terrible has happened. There are no witnesses whatsoever. One thing is for sure, Canada's well-known singer Martin Wilson didn't return from his concert in Vancouver today. If you have any information that might help the investigation, please call the number below . . ."

Victor turns the TV volume down and then turns it off. The World News Channel (WNC), which was just watching, always has the best news. They always seem to get the scoop.

He stares at the TV screen for a few seconds. Then he sets the remote back on the table, careful not to disturb Lucy.

His family doesn't really know much about him anyway, Victor thinks, setting Lucy's head on a pillow as he stands up. *It's time to remove Mr. Wilson from the trunk before he starts to stink.*

He leaves the room while singing calmly, his voice barely a whisper. "Strangers in the night, exchanging glances, wandering the night, what are the chances . . ." He continues whistling the same song, accompanied by the sound of footsteps going down the stairs . . .

CHAPTER 2

Alice Hill

It's a sunny day in Australia; nothing unusual about that. The "big yellow mate" is high in the sky. No clouds are around, and it's almost too hot to be outside. There's almost no wind.

Alice walks slowly. If you look carefully, you'll notice the excitement in her eyes. Her face says nothing. It has no expression, only her eyes. Those big blue eyes with which not even the cloudless sky can compete.

Gradually, a shadow crawls over her feet, up her small waist, and finally over her beautiful golden hair, which barely touches her shoulders. The shadow is created by a luxurious and elegant building. It looks like a pyramid made of glass.

As she approaches, the automatic door opens, and she walks inside.

"Good afternoon, Mrs. Hill!" a man says from the reception desk.

Alice nods and continues walking toward the elevator. Like everything else in the building, the elevator is also made of glass.

In no time, the elevator car arrives. As she walks inside, she pulls a red plastic card from her skirt and places it in a digital button that says "10."

A few seconds later, the door opens. As she walks out, she hears a voice.

"Hi, sugar, great to see you!" Her husband, David, can't hide his excitement even for a bit.

"How is the smartest man in the whole universe?" Alice asks, pressing her body against his. It makes her boobs look even bigger against the pressure of David's firm stomach.

He almost loses himself in that view, his imagination already playing games with him, when she pulls away.

"What's cookin'?" Alice asks while scanning the laboratory with her big blue eyes.

"Take a ten-minute break, guys," David says. "We'll continue shortly." He knows she doesn't like his employees staring at her.

In addition to being attractive, she's also popular on Instagram, having over two million followers. Mostly, she posts pictures of her travels and restaurants that she visits, but the most popular posts are pictures where she poses for the camera. Alice is twenty-five years old and gorgeous, and the camera loves her. There's no bad angle for Alice. No matter how the picture is taken, she looks stunning.

The laboratory is huge. Everything is white—the surfaces, the ceilings, even David and his employees' uniforms. David is the lead scientist and general manager of the facility. He's the main guy in the pyramid-shaped glass building called V & V99. They conduct futuristic medical experiments and revolutionary treatments that involve vitamins and viruses. The goal is to create viruses that will act positively in people's bodies and end people's need for vitamins, with the viruses able to produce any vitamins that the body lacks.

Say, for example, someone is starting to feel sick, and fever is flowing through the person's body. Instead of consuming lemon and honey, the person's body is a few steps ahead. Upon the first signs of such a virus, it produces vitamin C and all other necessary vitamins in large amounts. Then the person wakes up the next morning feeling healthy without having used any medicine or supplements.

The products are yet to be approved, but a few other products have made the company famous and made David Hill a rich and popular person around the world but especially in Australia.

"I feel like a hamster on a wheel," David says, letting out a huge sigh.

"Why's that?" Alice asks while making a childish face.

"Same damn story as a few months earlier. If the mixture of ingredients is off by just 0.01 percent, the host will die in a few weeks or even hours, depending on the amount of product they consume. I'm trying to save the people with this experiment, not kill them."

"You're a genius," Alice says with strength in her voice and her hand folded into a fist. "You'll figure it out. I believe in you; you know that!"

"Well, that's the main thing that's pushing me," he says. "Your support!"

He's a mature man in his early fifties with gray hair and gray eyebrows. He's tall and is in great shape for his age.

It's hard to say who has the "better deal," Alice or David. She's young and attractive, and he's smart, handsome, and rich.

"You know I like it when you show me how you make your elixirs," she says. "Come on, just for a few minutes!" She's acting like a child who's asking her parents to go to Disneyland.

"Alright, but no photos for Instagram or any other social media." He can never say no to Alice. He's crazy about her. Also, he feels powerful and proud of being able to show her his knowledge and skills. That's what he's best at.

"See this volumetric flask?" David says, beginning his tour. "It's filled with a golden liquid, like your hair."

Alice nods. Her massive blue eyes on the flask. "M-hmm . . ."

"Now I add just a drop of Vitolicerin 12, and behold!" The liquid in the flask turns purple and then freezes into purple ice.

Alice's eyebrows shoot up. "Wow! It's like magic!"

David smiles. "Exactly! But then—" Before he can finish, the door opens, and one of his employees, Mike, pokes his head into the room.

"Dr. Hill, someone just called from the police." He's hesitant to continue, unsure if he should speak with Alice there.

"Continue, please," David says, stepping toward Mike. "What happened?"

"It's Carlos, the guy from security. You know how he didn't show up for work yesterday? Anyway, they just called to let us know they found him dead in his house!"

"But . . . but why?" David asks, holding his hands in the air and looking at Mike for an answer. "He was a good man, young and healthy. What happened?"

I happened, Alice says to herself while, behind her back, she puts the tiny flask filled with Vitolicerin 12 into her purse.

CHAPTER 3

Bogdan Morozov

"Pass it! Pass it now!" one of the soccer players screams.

Bogdan ignores him while producing a fantastic dribble. He loses his opponent with his marvelous speed. Now it's only the goalkeeper to beat! Swinging his left foot back and preparing to launch the ball in the top-left corner, he stops his foot a few centimeters before it touches the ball while the goalkeeper throws himself to his right. As the goalkeeper falls, he sees the hidden curve on the side of Bogdan's lips. Bogdan was waiting for that! As the goalkeeper touches the grass, Bogdan takes a step closer and then kicks the ball in the opposite side of the goal. The fans go crazy, and all his teammates run toward him. They hug him and jump on his back, showering him with compliments from all sides.

"Amazing, man!"

"Great goal!"

"Dude, fantastic! Well done!"

Bogdan wipes the sweat from his forehead while looking at the stadium scoreboard, which says "FC Tom Tomsk 1; FC Baltika 0." It's the ninety-second minute, and the game is almost over. The moment Baltika's player passes the ball from the center, the referee blows the whistle, ending the game.

It's a sunny day in Tomsk, Russia, and the fans are still singing as the players head toward locker rooms after greeting and exchanging shirts with their rivals.

Bogdan undresses and then walks into the shower. It's a big area with more than twenty showerheads.

"That was a great goal, brother," his teammate says with a strong Russian accent while putting hair conditioner on his hairy dick.

"If you don't shave soon, you're going to lose him under that forest," Bogdan says, smiling as the rest of the team laughs.

"What? My girlfriend loves it!" Sergei says proudly.

"Maybe she likes to play hide-and-seek," says Ivan, another player, on his way out. The room explodes with laughter.

"Ha ha! Motherfucker!" Sergei says. "Come here, I'll fuck you in the ass!" He's yelling like a lunatic, but he still thinks the joke is funny.

Once everyone else finishes showering, Bogdan remains standing under the hot water, his eyes closed and not moving a muscle. He's the last man left in the locker room.

Bogdan loves the silence. The steam from the hot water is everywhere, and water slides off his bald head, over his face, and down his muscular, athletic body. The drops slide left and right on his skin as if trying to avoid all his tattoos like a skier on a mountain.

He loves staying with his own thoughts, but not for too long. The more he thinks, the more he goes into that dark place where he doesn't want to go. Who are his parents, and why did they leave him when he was just a baby?

Bogdan often thinks about that, of his childhood spent in an orphanage in Russia. He can't understand what he did wrong and what circumstances could make someone abandon their son like that. The more he allows himself to think about that, the angrier he gets and the more lost he feels. He's thirty years old now, but those thoughts still bother him.

Having finally had enough, he turns off the water.

Outside the stadium, he heads toward a taxi station.

"Which one is first to go?" Bogdan asks one of the taxi drivers, who is standing outside and smoking a cigarette. He points to the red car on his right.

Bogdan nods and then gets inside the cab. "To Peter Kazim Street, please."

The driver glances back at him. "That's an hour from here!"

Bogdan shrugs. "Well, more money for you, my friend."

The driver turns on his meter, puts on his seatbelt, and starts driving.

The weather is nice, but it's getting colder, and in around an hour, it will be dark.

Bogdan opens his sports bag and looks inside. He raises his head and looks to the left, right, and then in the rear-view mirror and sees a black SUV behind them.

Good, they're following, he thinks, making himself comfortable. "Brother," he says to the driver, "you have any music?"

The driver turns on the radio and catches the end of one of Bogdan's favorite songs, "Sweet Dreams," the Marilyn Manson version. "I'm gonna use you and abuse you; I'm gonna know what's inside you . . ." Bogdan loves heavy metal. It helps to calm him.

After almost an hour, they arrive at his destination.

"Just here on the left, brother," Bogdan says. "Behind that grey van."

It's dark, and nothing is there except the grey van. It looks like an abandoned area, quite scary. Only one streetlamp is working, and it goes on and off constantly. The taxi driver takes his money and then leaves straight away.

Bogdan crouches next to the streetlight and opens his bag. At that moment, five people walk slowly toward him. They are the guys from the black SUV. They parked not far from there, turned their headlights off, and waited for a taxi driver to go.

"Hi kid," says one of the men, Andrei, as he casually lays a baseball bat on his shoulder. "How are you doing?"

Bogdan turns around and scans all of them. *Hmm . . . two knives and three baseball bats . . .*

"Nobody refuses to play for my club!" Andrei says. "I gave you a good offer. I want to make you a star, but you're a stubborn idiot, and I have a reputation to maintain. Nobody says no to me! When I'm finished with you, the only soccer you'll be playing is on the fucking PlayStation!" His voice echoes in the darkness around them.

Andrei keeps yelling, but Bogdan isn't listening. Instead, he closes his eyes and starts whispering.

"What's that?" Andrei says, stepping closer. "It's too late for praying!"

"Some of them want to use you . . ." Bogdan sings under his breath. The others can barely hear him, but in his head, he can still hear the song from the taxi. "Some of them want to be used by you . . ." He starts moving his head up and down slowly and then faster and faster like the song is actually playing out loud, but it's all in his head, in his dark place. His eyes are still closed.

"There's nowhere to run," Andrei says. "This is it!" Spreading his arms wide, he walks toward Bogdan.

Bogdan is holding something in his hands: a wire from the streetlamp. The moment they are close enough, he cuts the wire, and everything is swallowed by darkness.

Bogdan opens his eyes, which are now almost completely used to the dark, seeing as they were closed for so long. He watches as they start panicking and yelling, swinging their bats and almost hitting one other.

Like a predator approaching his prey, Bogdan leaps at them. He grabs a guy with a knife from behind and breaks his neck.

Bogdan snatches the guy's knife and rushes to the next guy, who is swinging his baseball bat all over the place. Bogdan slides into the guy's ankles, knocking him down. The moment the guy touches the ground, the last thing he feels is the strong, sharp pain of the cold knife slicing his throat before he chokes on his own blood.

Bogdan finishes the next two guys with fast, precise throat cuts as well. He can't risk sparing more time before their eyes adjust to the dark as well.

Only Andrei is left, swinging his bat through the darkness and not knowing what's happening around him. Bogdan stands for a moment.

"Now I see you!" Andrei screams. "I'm gonna fucking kill you!"

Bogdan presses a button on his car keys, and the grey van's high beams turn on, blinding Andrei and shocking his eyes once again. He swings his bat once more and then falls to the ground.

Bogdan walks slowly toward him and puts his right foot on the baseball bat, pressing it into the ground, not allowing Andrei to lift it. Andrei lifts his head and sees the rest of his gang is dead.

"What . . . what's happening?" Andrei asks. "This isn't possible. Who are you? I have lots of money. Tell me how much." As he says this, he shakes like a wet dog on a cold night.

"Money?" Bogdan asks. "Why, so I can buy a fucking PlayStation?"

The moment the words are out of his mouth, he grabs Andrei's head and jams the knife through his eye socket and out the back of his skull.

CHAPTER 4

Grandpa Luigi's House

Victor grew up without his parents. They separated shortly after he was born and are currently living in the US with different partners. He has never spoken with them or about them, and for him, they are complete strangers.

His Grandma Olivia and Grandpa Luigi took care of him. Though he loves them both, Grandpa Luigi was his favorite. He was a black-haired Italian who spent half of his life in Italy and half in Canada. Italy was the main topic in every one of Grandpa Luigi's conversations.

Victor still lives in the same house in which he grew up with them. Victor spent his entire childhood with them; they were inseparable! That is, when Grandpa Luigi was at home—he traveled a lot.

Grandpa Luigi was Victor's mentor and best friend until he passed away five years ago, just a year after Grandma Olivia left this world. It was the hardest period of Victor's life. He was dating Lucy at the time, and if it weren't for her, it would be questionable whether he could have made it through that hell. Of course, together with "Puppy Leo," who was his last gift from Grandpa Luigi.

As Victor goes down the stairs, Leo approaches, and Victor gently touches his head as an acknowledgment of his presence and then continues toward the garage door. That's the end of the road for Leo. He knows the garage is the only area in the entire house where he isn't allowed.

When Victor goes to the garage, even Lucy knows not to bother him. That's where he does his planning and projects for the restaurant or just relaxes by adding some small touches to his car. He loves his time alone there.

As he enters and turns on the lights, his black Jeep Grand Cherokee 2007 is revealed in front of him. It's a great family car that he has owned for many years.

He approaches from the back and opens his trunk. In front of him is a big black wheeled plastic container. Victor uses a ramp to wheel the container out of the trunk. Then he closes the trunk and steps on a rectangular metal plate with the container next to him.

He presses a red button, and then he begins descending on a mini elevator. It leads to a pit under the car that allows Victor to check parts of the vehicle that are hard to reach otherwise.

Such a feature is quite usual in this part of the world, especially considering the house was built many years ago. Victor uses the pit for mechanical work, but something much deeper and darker is hiding down there.

The pit is cold, dark, and oily, and there isn't anything else down there except an old white plastic wall phone. Victor lifts the handset and presses some numbers, then returns the handset to its cradle. Shortly after that, he hears a click from somewhere inside the pit. He pushes the wall, and a small door that's about the same size as the black plastic container opens. Victor opens the container, revealing a black plastic bag with Mr. Wilson's body inside.

He tips one side of the container up, and the body slides down through the hole.

He picks up the headset again and presses some numbers. Then he feels but doesn't hear an engine starting behind the wall. It's mincing Mr. Wilson's body before distributing it to the river nearby via a series of underground pipes, where it will be eaten by fish.

Victor is silent as he stares at a single spot. All he can hear is his own breathing.

It's his eleventh murder.

CHAPTER 5

"Sounds Like A Plan"

"Honey, is everything alright?" Alice asks as they walk home. David is looking into the distance as he tries to solve a puzzle in his head.

"What? Sorry, I mean, I'm shocked. He was a young man. Why would anyone—"

"Sweetie, I know it's terrible, but I'm sure the police will find whoever did this and make him pay!" She places her left hand on his shoulder and tries to turn his body toward her. "Can we talk about something else now?"

David sighs. "Oh, okay. You're right. How are things? Anything new?"

"Actually, I need to travel to Indonesia, Bali in particular, to make some pictures and videos for my Instagram page regarding something that's going on with social media at the moment. Should I bother to ask you to go with me?"

"Don't be like that, sweetie. You know I would, but I've never been closer to finalizing this project. If I pull this off, I won't need to work for the rest of my life, and we can travel wherever you want!"

"Sounds like a plan!" Alice says. Her voice sounds encouraging, but in truth, she doesn't want him to come. He would only interfere with her mission, which is the last thing she wants. That guy, Carlos from security, knew what it meant to interfere in Alice's mission, and now he's dead.

Carlos saw her taking the biggest volumetric flask full of the elixir that David was working on from the lab. She was mad at herself. It was a beginner's mistake, and she isn't a beginner; no sir. Carlos stopped her and asked to have a look in her bag. It happened in the main lab, the only place without cameras. That was why she had lowered her guard. She hadn't expected Carlos to walk in and see her. She pulled out a small bottle of perfume and sprayed his face. "It's just my perfume, see? Now get lost before my husband walks in and fires you!" Carlos didn't know what to do. He started apologizing and saying it was an honest mistake; he had loved his job since the day he came from Mexico, that it had been the light at the end of the tunnel for him and his family . . . She waved rapidly in his direction, motioning for him to get out of her sight.

Carlos left for home that day, hoping that everything would be alright, and she would not tell Dr. David, but he couldn't imagine that was the last thing he should have been worried about.

The perfume bottle was filled with Vitolicerin 12 elixir. One sniff, and a person will be dead in a few hours or within a couple of days, depending on the individual. Carlos never saw it coming. He was never a mission; he was just a guy who was in the wrong place at the wrong time.

"So, when do you need to go?" David asks.

"Tomorrow morning, actually, but it's only for three days!"

David's face falls. "Oh, that soon . . ."

"I don't want to distract you from your project, and it's normal for me to travel a few times a month. It'll be good for you to focus on your work for the next three days. Maybe when I come back, the serum will be done!" She knows what she's doing, encouraging him and making it look like it's in his favor for her to go on a trip.

David smiles at her. "I'm going to miss you too much." He grabs her face with both hands and kisses her on the lips.

CHAPTER 6

The Russian Mob

For Alice, going to Bali awakens a lot of memories. She used to go there often with her friends because she loves the sun, the beach, bikinis, and of course, surfing.

Her plane lands at Ngurah Rai Airport in the midst of a strong summer rain that will probably pass in half an hour. The flight was bumpy, one of the most turbulent flights Alice has ever had. The pilot sang a song upon landing, "Can't Help Falling In Love" by Elvis Presley. She found it very amusing. She remembers a guy who she met in Bali a few years earlier. It was their song at that time, so she becomes emotional with this coincidence. *Where is he now?* She wonders. *Nah. Don't be a softy, Alice. That was a long time ago.*

A taxi drops her in the southernmost area of the island, called Uluwatu. Her accommodation is a simple family home, rented out by a friendly Indonesian family. It has a single room and a toilet, and that's it. Of course, people don't travel to Bali because of its luxury accommodations. Everything outside of accommodation is pure gold when it comes to natural beauty, peace, and beaches. However, Alice isn't there for any of those things. She has arrived for something much bigger.

Alice pulls out her phone and swipes the screen. Amidst the many photo editing applications and a few games is an app called "The Nobodies."

She taps her finger, and the phone opens one of the stupidest arcade games ever. But she's not there for playing. She taps "Options" and then "About us." The screen displays the following message: "Please enter the four-digit code provided."

Most people who download this game, which is very unpopular, would not click on "About us." Most likely, they would delete it immediately because the game is such a disaster. But that's the point. It's not a game; it's a way to communicate.

She enters the four-digit code that's unique to her, and the phone goes to the "Description" page. Under that, she sees several pictures of people's faces accompanied by the following text: "Hello, Nobody. Your next mission is Russian arms dealer Cheslav Egorov. He's currently on vacation in Indonesia, in the area called Kuta. He has eight of his most loyal people with him. He likes the Forbidden Fruits nightclub, one of the biggest and most popular clubs in Kuta."

The text is quite long, and it contains lots of sentences that begin with "He likes," "He has," and "He would." His habits and movements are also quite detailed. Everything she needs to know is there.

Alice studies the text for over two hours, paper and pen in hand. She's completely focused on planning before she falls asleep at around 11:00 a.m. She needs the rest. Tonight is the night.

"Ivan! Bring more vodka for the boys!" Cheslav yells with a strong Russian accent. "The night just started. This is our most successful year so far, and we're going to party Russian style!" He's sitting on the edge of a pool with his hairy legs under the water and his even hairier upper body above the surface.

"On it, boss!" Ivan says. He's happy they can spend and drink as much as they want until they pass out.

The party gets wilder by the minute. With all the ladies around the Russians, it's not hard to realize who is the richest at the party.

The DJ doesn't take any chances. He goes with the most popular songs around the globe. "Sexy Bitch" by David Guetta and Akon comes on, and the crowd goes wild.

The black-haired waitress arrives with nine Russian special shots on the tray, and the Russians start jumping around her to the beat of the song.

"This one is on the house, boys!" she says. She puts the shots between her boobs, and then they grab them with their mouths.

"Hey, you, waitress," Cheslav says, "come here! I want you!" His eyes are already wandering. He's drunk, but he's still standing.

"A Russian special for you, handsome?" she says. Taking the last shot, she puts it between her boobs and then beckons him closer with her fingers.

He stumbles left and right but manages to dive his face between her boobs, grabbing the shot and drinking it at once.

He shakes his head left and right. The taste of alcohol is strong, and he's close to puking, but he manages to focus on the waitress. "Why don't you remove your sunglasses, sexy? I want to see your eyes. Come on, it's dark already!"

She pulls the sunglasses a bit lower on her nose, revealing her big blue eyes. "It's just going to get darker, believe me." She waves and then disappears into the crowd.

Alice approaches the exit, pretending to be drunk and acting like she's having a conversation on her phone in Russian. Then she goes outside, gets on her scooter, and puts on her helmet.

Being an arms dealer and get killed by "shots" in the club. You must love the irony, Alice thinks as she guns her scooter and disappears into the night.

CHAPTER 7

The Nobodies Committee

A dark room. Somewhere. Three gentlemen and one lady are sitting at a square table. They are all in their fifties and sixties. One of them, Connor, a man with stylish grey hair, exhales. "So, as you all know by now, Cheslav Egorov and his crew were found dead in their hotel room on Bali."

"She did a great job," Vera says. "Black wig, pretending to be a waitress. I like her style." She sips the remainder of her vodka. She has small blue eyes, short white hair, and a somewhat mean face.

"He's a Russian, like you," says Pierre, a bald guy with a goatee and an abnormally large nose and ears. "Must be hard for you to say something like that." He loves to bug Vera about her nationality.

Vera sniffs. "He was a piece of shit. That's why he was on our list. If he were French, would you feel sorry for him?"

All three gentlemen smile.

"You're a strong woman," Gamba says. "Stronger than most men, but relax, Vera. Pierre isn't trying to provoke you, right Pierre?" Gamba is a black-skinned African with a grey mustache, a bit of white hair on the sides of the head, but completely bald on top.

They call themselves "The Nobodies." Without a doubt, they are the most dangerous organization in the world. When people hear the word "organization," most think of a big building with hundreds of employees, lots of weapons, and possibly an army, but The Nobodies are different.

For starters, there are only four of them. The only weapons they have are for self-defense, and they have no building or army.

However, their small size is their greatest power. With no building or army, no one can ever trace any of their crimes back to them.

Instead, they hire regular people with clean police records but with great potential using The Nobodies mobile game application, which they created a few years ago, to find them.

Candidates are carefully selected and observed for many months or even years, and some of them are children or grandchildren of previous assassins.

Every one of them is smart enough to know what will happen if they ever mention The Nobodies to anyone, even their families. But why would they when The Nobodies pay seven digits minimum for each mission, cash, delivered to the assassin's house?

The only bad part is, once someone joins The Nobodies, there's no way out. If someone is lucky and skilled, he or she can grow old and die as part of the group. But if anyone thinks they have made enough money and wants to exit the game, other assassins will be sent to finish them. Such people are a threat; they know too much.

Some have tried in the past, but they lost everything and everyone, including their own lives. The Nobodies have eyes and ears everywhere, and they know everything.

If one of their assassins goes to the toilet to take a piss, The Nobodies know which hand the person uses to hold his dick, how long it takes him to pee, and if he flushes.

Connor, Vera, Pierre, and Gamba are the four most dangerous people on the planet that no one has ever heard of.

They meet once a month, or more if necessary, always in a different location, casually discussing the murders that they have organized and what their next steps should be.

The Nobodies are shaping the world the way they want the world to be. They are trying to balance it. Whoever they want to live stays, and people who they think are not valuable enough or who are a potential threat go on the list, and everyone on the list ends up deep in the ground, in the river, or in a meat grinder.

The good thing is, they mostly kill bad people around the world. However, they also kill the occasional good person. They have their idea of a perfect world, and they strive to create that world from the shadows.

In the past, there were a couple more organizations similar to them, but The Nobodies eliminated them all, and now they are the only ones.

"What about that guy who killed that annoying child rapist singer Wilson in Vancouver?" Gamba asks. "What's his name, Victor? I mean killing him with the pen that he was signing autographs with, that was pretty cool."

For Gamba, who has been doing this with the others for over thirty years now, life and death are a cheerful topic. It's just a game for him, and it feels disconnected from real people. He's always smiling, stretching his grey mustache over his face. Deadly and unpredictable.

"Give me the statistics, Pierre, please," Connor says with a serious voice and an icy look in his handsome eyes. There are no leaders in this organization, but anyone in the same room as them sees the others treat Connor as their leader. He's also the one who started The Nobodies in the first place.

"Forty-six of forty-seven people on the list around the globe this week are dead," Pierre says, an unsatisfactory vibration in his voice.

"So, not one hundred percent?" Vera asks, narrowing her already small blue eyes as she looks at Connor.

"Yeah, that lieutenant from Paris is giving us a bit of a headache," Gamba says, his smile faltering for a moment.

Vera looks at Pierre. "You must be proud."

Pierre glares at her. "Oh, you've been waiting for this, haven't you?"

Connor raises his hand to stop their conversation. "Our assassin is dead. The lieutenant killed him, end of the story. I've already sent another, and this one will not make the same mistake."

"Who did you send?" Gamba asks.

"Emilio," Connor replies, his voice almost a whisper.

There's a moment of silence as Gamba, Pierre, and Vera look at one another.

"You really don't like Lieutenant Mercier, hmm?" Gamba asks.

Connor doesn't respond.

"Really," Pierre says. "Emilio . . ."

"Au revoir, Lieutenant," Vera says confidently while pouring another glass of vodka. All of them think of Emilio as a guy who always gets the job done.

"So we have twenty-six Nobodies left?" Gamba asks while stretching his mustache with his right hand. (They called their assassins Nobodies as well.)

Connor nods. "Correct. I think that some of them are becoming sloppy, so we might want to consider reducing that number to ten at most."

Vera looks at him. "Reducing that number? As in—"

"Eliminate sixteen Nobodies," Connor says. "It sounds harsh, I know, but that Nobody from Australia, Alice, she killed that security guard because she was sloppy, and she allowed him to see her. That sort of thing can cost us."

Gamba sat back in his chair. "Now, why would that be a good idea?"

"These people do what we ask them to do, and they're pretty good at it, don't you think?" Vera asks while rotating her glass clockwise. They have all been friends for decades, but Vera was the first one to join Connor when he began recruiting.

"I'm starting to think we have too many Nobodies," Connor says. "If you remember, we started with only four: us."

"But the more we have, the easier and faster it is to eliminate our targets around the globe," Pierre points out.

Connor shrugs. "Maybe, but the more Nobodies we have, the more Ears and Eyes we need to hire. And we have lots of them too, wouldn't you agree?"

"Ears" and "Eyes" are the people hired by The Nobodies to follow their assassins' every single step and report back to them. They are not killers, and they are not allowed to kill anybody even in self-defense. Killing is for the Nobodies only. The Ears and Eyes are also the ones who deliver the money to the Nobodies upon successfully completed task, bags full of cash.

"So what you're saying is that we have too many people, and you're afraid that one of them will make a mistake that leads to us or compromises our committee?" Pierre asks.

"I'm not afraid, my dearest friend," Connor says. "Our committee is so unbelievably important to this world's existence that we should remove any possibility of putting us in danger in any way."

Vera nodded slowly, "Fair enough. I'll consider what you've just said and let you know my opinion at our next meeting."

Pierre stands up. "Gents and the lady, until we meet again."

"Alright," Gamba says, "see you soon."

In general, they are "good" dangerous people, not the type to kill for no reason or for personal greed.

Connor doesn't see killing sixteen Nobodies as an evil act. To him, it's a just act, ensuring that the committee will live for many more years, which means lots of bad people will die, making the world a better place.

He has planted the idea in their heads, but if they don't all agree, it will not go forward.

CHAPTER 8

Time For The Gym

It's August 7, 2018, and Victor is saying goodbye to Lucy and Leo at the Vancouver Airport. He's going to San Francisco, California, to help with a restaurant opening there. At least that's what he told Lucy. In truth, he has a new target.

"See you soon, my love," Victor says. "And you as well, Leo. Take care of Mama!" He waves goodbye while heading toward the doors.

"Don't forget that picnic you promised!" Lucy says, pointing at him to let him know she hasn't forgotten about the promise he made to her, so she would let him go on this trip.

"Picnic, baby! Woo-hoo!" Victor says before vanishing into the airport.

Once the plane is in the air, Victor thinks about his target, Daniel Newman. He's an American businessman, who is, according to The Nobodies, involved in a large number of crimes, including drugs, child pornography, rape, and murder.

Usually, Victor's targets are located in Canada or even British Columbia, making it easy for him to dispose of the bodies in his garage. Now he needs to think of something else. Also, this is his second mission in two months. They aren't usually that often.

Victor is a bit nervous about the mission. He'll be in a different country under different circumstances. It crosses his mind that if the missions are to become harder and more often, he will have a hard time maintaining his double life. He could also lose Lucy's trust if he travels too often; it could smell like an affair.

I wish, he thinks. It would be easier to explain an affair than what he's actually doing.

His brain is going on and on with all the possibilities and solutions when the pilot announces it's time to buckle up and prepare for landing. Victor decides that from that moment he needs to think only about the mission. He can't allow anything to distract him and cause him to make a mistake.

He arrives at his hotel in San Francisco, takes a shower, and then speaks with Lucy over Skype, telling her that tomorrow morning he will go to the restaurant because it's already 1:00 a.m., and he's going to go to sleep.

Victor created a plan at home the moment he received the message in The Nobodies app. As always, it included a detailed explanation of the target's likes and dislikes together with the target's possible movements and meetings.

Victor decides to do it at the gym because it's the only place on the list that doesn't have cameras. However, it's also risky. Everything needs to go according to plan, or Victor could be caught.

Newman is in his early fifties. He has blond hair and an old face, but his pointed nose is the first thing anyone notices about him. He loves to work out in plain white clothes and to talk with other guys who train there.

Victor enters Supreme Gym and signs up for a day pass. Then he examines the gym to see how it's equipped.

Good, he thinks. *Exactly the same as it was described in the app.*

"You're good to go, Mr. Philips. Have a good one!" A guy whose nametag says "Jake" gives the pass to Victor. Of course, Victor used a fake name, and there is no need to use an ID for a day pass.

Victor thanks the attendant and then walks deeper into the gym. A guy near him is exercising his biceps, but it's not Newman.

Victor spots Newman doing the deadlift in the far corner of the gym and starts walking toward him. When he's close enough, he chooses a leg machine that's just two meters away from Newman and starts exercising his legs. Exercising his legs means no fingerprints.

Out of the corner of his eye, Victor observes Newman's movements and behavior. He's an old guy, but it looks like he's in fine shape.

"Big mistake, young man!" Newman says, waggling his index finger at Victor.

"What? Excuse me?" Victor is a bit caught off guard even though he knows that Newman is quite an engaging person.

"Never start without stretching and warming up your muscles!" Newman says. "That's kind of a basic, don't you think?" As a senior and the oldest guy in the gym, Newman likes to give lessons and speeches to the other guys, who are sometimes even three times younger than him.

"Oh, that, yeah, I know, valid point," Victor says. "Couldn't agree more with you Mr. . . .?"

"Newman, but you can call me Danny as everyone else here in the gym does." He wants to shake Victor's hand, but Victor folds his hand into a fist instead for a fist bump.

"Sorry, but my hand is wet," Victor says. "Outside it's like a million degrees. I'm Josh. Pleasure to meet you." Newman smiles. He's in a good mood. It's noon, so the gym is quite empty, just one more guy and the gym attendant.

"As I was saying," Victor continues, "you're right. It's just that I have lots on my list for today, so I'm kinda in a hurry." Little does Newman realize that the main thing on Victor's list is him.

Victor's trains for as long as Newman trains, and then they got to the locker room at the same time.

"Wish I had more time to do a bit more intense training," Victor says.

"You know what they say," Newman replies. "Any training is better than no training at all." He hangs up his white training clothes, grabs a white towel, and starts walking toward the showers.

"Right." Victor grabs a towel and walks a few meters behind Newman.

Adrenaline runs through his body as he reviews his plan in his head. Never before has he connected with a victim before killing them . Is this guy really that bad? Does he deserve to die? Victor has read all the info about him on the app, but suddenly he doubts it. He feels a bit insecure. Tons of different emotions run through his body, but one thought is stronger than the others: if he doesn't do it, he and Lucy will be the next target. He has no choice.

"Why are you so quiet, boy?" Newman asks once they're in the shower. "This hot water putting you asleep?" As he says this, his tilts his head back and closes his eyes, so the shower massages his face, giving himself over completely to that pleasurable feeling.

Victor doesn't answer him. He merely whispers "I'm sorry" and then wraps his towel around his left fist and strikes Newman in the forehead. He hits him so hard that Newman's head hits the wall behind him, and he falls over. Victor catches him, wraps the same towel around his face, and lies back on the floor, with Newman on his chest facing the ceiling, making the water fall directly on the towel and block the oxygen flow. Newman struggles, but he's still in shock from his head hitting the wall. He waves his arms, but it's slow, uncontrolled, and hopeless. Eventually, his arms fall, and he draws his last breath.

Victor doesn't hesitate for a second. He uses the same towel to rub-down the parts of Newman's body that he touched during the murder.

He also wipes the part of the wall that Newman hit with his head. There's no blood, but just in case. He grabs some soap and rubs it on Newman's feet, then leaves the soap on the floor, trying to make it look as much like an accident as possible.

He stands there for a moment. The showers are still running, and steam is crawling into the room, making him sweat even more. It's over. He turns to walk out of the shower room.

Out of nowhere, the guy who was exercising his biceps earlier jumps on Victor and cuts his left arm with a knife. Victor is confused and caught off guard but is conscious enough to wrap the towel around his arm once again, this time to prevent any blood from dropping on the floor. He doesn't want to leave a trace of his presence.

The guy swings his knife up and down, left and right, which reveals he isn't very skilled with it. Victor waits for the guy to go for his stomach. Then he uses his left hand, which is still wrapped in the towel, to redirect his swing and punches the elbow of the arm that's holding the knife. With Victor putting pressure on the guy's hand, he stabs himself in the chest.

Some of the guy's blood gets on the towel wrapped around Victor's arm. He pushes the man's body off himself. *Where did he come from, and what connection does he has with Newman?* he wonders. *Is this his bodyguard or what?*

This is no time for piecing the puzzle together. He needs to think. How can he make this look like an accident or something else? He looks behind him and sees Newman on the floor, water from the shower still falling on his dead-white face. He turns around and sees the guy with the knife in his chest. Victor yanks the knife out of the guy's chest with the towel wrapped around his hand, then goes to Newman and places it in his right hand and puts pressure on Newman's hand, ensuring all the fingerprints on the knife are Newman's.

It's hard to imagine what kind of story the police will pull out of this one, but with all the water falling, cleaning away the evidence, and considering this is a gym and lots of people take showers there each day, the number of fingerprints, hairs, and other traces will be countless.

Victor dresses as quickly as possible, hoping no one else will enter the locker room.

He takes his bag and is about to leave when he turns around and scans the room one last time. Something isn't right about the situation. *That guy wasn't supposed to attack me at any stage because if he was just a regular man having a daily workout, seeing me kill Newman should have scared him and made him run away, but instead, he charged me. This wasn't just a daily workout for him, I'm sure.*

Two training bags are in the locker room. Above one is Newman's white clothes, which means the other bag is from the guy with the knife. Victor opens the bag carefully using some surgical gloves that he always carries in his pocket.

A phone, that's what he's searching for. He presses the iPhone's home button, and it asks him to enter a password. "Fuck it." Victor dashes back to the shower room, grabs the dead guy's right hand, and places his thumb on the home button, unlocking the phone. He opens the menu and wants to go into the man's messages, but one thing seizes his attention.

The Nobodies application. He's stunned.

With a serious face, he approaches the attendant at the front desk.

Jake smiles as he approaches. "How can I h—" His voice is cut off as Victor grabs him by the neck.

"Cut the bullshit! Tell them I'm coming for them!" He pushes Jake away and then leaves the phone on the attendant's desk.

There is no way that "Jake" isn't playing a part in the story. This wasn't a setup for Newman. It was a setup for Victor.

CHAPTER 9

The Picnic

Victor flies back to Vancouver that night at 11:00 p.m. Throughout the flight, all he can think about is what the next setup will be. The adrenaline has faded, and fear has crawled under his skin. He knows how dangerous the people who are leading The Nobodies operations are. He should not have told "Jake" that he was coming after them. That was stupid.

Victor doesn't even know who "they" are. Now he's thinking of Lucy. Is she safe?

Thankfully, she is. The day after he arrives home, they drive for around 4.5 hours before they reach a place called Pemberton and park their car in the day-use lot. Victor gets out of the car together with Lucy and Leo, and they all stretch after the long drive.

"Well, from this location, there's a 2.5-hour hike until we reach the third lake."

"I can definitely use a walk," Lucy says. "I hope Joffre Lake is as magical as everyone says."

Victor smiles. "Well, if we liked it on Google, I'm sure it will be even more amazing in person."

Before they realize it, Leo leaves the car and is happy to release one of the biggest dog poops by far.

Lucy sighs. "I'll clean it up, honey. You grab the backpacks, and let's roll!"

The hike is fun and exciting, and it doesn't feel like 2.5 hours. They enjoy being together and also watching Leo running in front of them and checking out the territory.

Leo isn't a regular European Doberman. He's a Supreme Doberman, the largest kind of Doberman. They can weigh over 120 lbs or 60 kg. He's a tall, huge, muscular dog, but he also has outstanding character. He loves even the smallest animals, like rabbits and cats. That doesn't mean he lacks the famous guardian blood that Dobermans have. When he feels that something or someone is a danger, he becomes sharp and fearless. Just the way he looks in those moments will repel anyone who is thinking of trying anything.

Leo is well equipped for this trip. He has a leather collar with silver spikes that match his black spiked harness. He looks like a gladiator. Victor likes Leo to wear such gear when they go deep into woods. He says they never know when they'll encounter a bear, a cougar, or a pack of coyotes, so at least he has some kind of protection.

Victor is well aware that the chance of something like that happening is slim. The truth is, he likes how Leo looks dressed like that. Victor loves Leo with the same amount of love that he has for Lucy. Leo is his best friend forever.

They pass a waterfall and take a few pictures that Lucy posts on Facebook straight away. It's like a dream. The lake is exceptionally blue, the views are stunning, and the mountains have some snow on the top, even though it's summer. The trees are green and beautiful, and a light breeze slides through their hair.

They sit on a red blanket with a small fire in front of them, hugging each other as they look at the lake. Leo is lying next to them.

"This is what life should be about," Victor says.

"What do you mean?" Lucy whispers.

"Enjoying the simple things with the people you care about." He almost sounds poetic.

Lucy looks at him. "Isn't that what life is right now?"

"People don't care about simple things anymore," Victor says. "Greed has poisoned people's souls."

Lucy scowls. "Where's that coming from?" She nudges him. "Relax, and enjoy this moment."

"Yeah, right. I'm sorry." He rubs his right hand on Leo's fur.

"I don't want to break your poetic moment, but I really need to pee," Lucy says. She stands up, but before she leaves, she stops for a moment and looks at Victor.

"What?" Victor says. "Sorry. I'll stop being so pessimistic."

She turns without another word and disappears into the woods.

It's sunset. The night is falling fast, and soon the most visible thing is the small fire that they lit earlier that day.

Victor's head is full of thoughts. He stops thinking for a moment when he realizes it has been more than a few minutes since Lucy left. She should be back by now. He stands up.

"Lucy?" He listens for a moment. "Lucy!" He begins to shake as he considers the worst-possible scenario. He shouldn't have been rude to The Nobodies. They might have Lucy now. He has no idea what's happening.

He sees movement behind a tree. Leo stands up and starts growling.

"Lucy? Are you alrig—" Before he can finish, a big gray wolf appears from the dark.

Victor inches backward to reach the knife in his backpack. More wolves appear; they're surrounded. *How can this be?* he wonders. *No one ever sees wolves in this area. And where the hell is Lucy?*

Victor counts five gray wolves and one dark-gray wolf that's noticeably bigger than the others, probably the leader of the pack. Victor considers attacking the alpha wolf, but he's too far from his backpack. The wolves will eat his face before he can get to it.

One of the gray wolves rushes toward Victor, and he raises his arms to protect his neck and face, but Leo grabs the wolf by the neck and tackles him to the ground.

Victor doesn't hesitate. He runs toward his backpack to grab his knife.

The other four wolves jump on Leo and start biting his legs and neck. Victor reaches his backpack, pulls out his big hunting knife, then runs toward the wolves. He wants to kick the fire toward them, but then he realizes it's the only light he has, so he jumps over it and swings his knife at the wolves. They back off for a moment, except for the wolf that Leo grabbed by the neck. He has trouble standing up, and Victor seizes the opportunity to slice the wolf's throat.

Leo isn't in the best shape. His spiked collar and harness protected him from some bites, but he has a few cuts on his legs and back. Victor and Leo stand next to each other, not ready to give up just yet. But with five wolves left, Victor doesn't like the odds.

"Leo, stay strong!" Victor says. "We can win this!" He has always believed that Leo can understand him.

Leo bares his teeth and walks slowly toward the wolves.

"Leo, no! Stay here! Leo!" Victor screams, but Leo continues straight toward the alpha wolf.

They stand in front of each other. Leo is big, alpha wolf is bigger.

They stand on the hind legs and start wrestling and trying to grab each other's necks. Victor rushes to help, but the other four wolves block his path.

One of the wolves jumps on Victor, and he falls onto his back. He raises his left arm to protect his neck, and the wolf bites his arm instead. The pain is indescribable.

Realizing he's still holding the knife in his right hand, Victor stabs the wolf multiple times through the ribs.

He stands up as fast as he can, barely able to use his left arm.

Victor looks toward where the big fight is happening, and he can't believe his eyes. His favorite "gladiator" harness and collar seem to have given some advantage to Leo. The alpha wolf has trouble biting Leo, the spikes damaging his gums.

He manages to bite Leo in the legs and on the back, but Leo grabs the wolf's neck and face. The alpha wolf backs down. He's in bad shape. He turns and runs into the woods.

Leo turns his attention toward other wolves. They back up slowly. They already tried to bite him earlier, and they remember the pain from the spikes.

Victor gives support to Leo by running with him toward the other wolves, and they turn around and vanish into the woods. Victor almost cries in happiness until he turns around and sees Leo lying down.

Victor rushes toward him. The light from the fire reveals bites and cuts all over Leo's body. There are many; blood is everywhere. In the dark, Leo's black fur hid his injuries well, but now it's clear. Some of the alpha wolf's bites reached Leo's neck and ribs.

"What's happening?" Victor cries. "God, what is this? Leo, hang in there, man, don't give up!" He hugs Leo with both arms, soaking his shirt with blood.

Leo's eyes look sad. He looks directly into Victor's eyes as if to ask, "Have I done well?"

Victor bursts into tears. He feels like something is pressing on his chest, and he can't breathe.

He passes out next to Leo as the fire burns out, leaving them both in total darkness.

CHAPTER 10

What A Friendly Pub

It has been a couple of weeks since the night that Bogdan took five lives.

He's a bit surprised that he just got another task because it's never happened so soon, but he considers himself a professional, and he will complete whatever task is given to him no matter what.

Bogdan is already in Kiev, Ukraine's capital. He's sitting on a bench sipping a local energy drink called Revo. He's wearing a black leather jacket, black pants, and black boots. People might think he's a so-called "skinhead," but Bogdan just likes to wear black clothes.

He finishes his drink and squeezes the can, then turns and throws it into the bin.

The night is falling, and he's been on the bench for a few hours when he decides it's time to go. He gets up and walks toward a pub called Tin, which translates as "Shadow."

The pub has a bad reputation. It's a meeting point for many petty criminals and sometimes major criminals. They are sitting at the same table as police officers on duty, including captains and commissioners. Everybody knows about it, but nobody cares. It's an open secret, but the situation in the country is so bad that it's hard to say who are good and who are the bad people and what defines them.

When Bogdan reaches the front of the pub, two big-fat security guards stop him.

"What do you want?" one of them asks in Ukrainian.

"I'm here to hide from my shadow," Bogdan replies, also in Ukrainian.

That sentence is the password to let him into the pub. It means someone important knows him or is inside to meet him. The Nobodies application granted this information to Bogdan, as per usual. The security guard opens the door and lets him in.

The bar is playing some Ukrainian/Russian rock music while the bearded bartender pours vodka, some of the customers play billiards, and others talk too loudly or too quietly.

Bogdan sits at the bar and orders a double vodka on ice. He rarely drinks, but he feels too stiff and is a bit worried that others will notice that and blew his cover. He finishes half of the pour in the first sip and then places the glass in front of him.

"Ukrainian or Russian?" the bartender asks while polishing a wine glass.

Bogdan: "Well I . . ."

"It doesn't make any difference to me, boy." The bartender has long hair on the sides and back of his head, but the top is bald.

"Russian," Bogdan says. "I have some family here. Just visiting" He turns around slowly and looks for his target.

"Well, you won't find them in here," the bartender says.

"No, just looking to see if there's a free spot at the billiard table. Love the game."

"They just finished the game over there," the bartender says. "Better go before they start a new one."

"Right, thanks!" Bogdan says. After finishing his drink, he leaves some money on the bar and then goes toward the area with the billiard tables. He walks slowly and looks around, but he still can't spot his target. "You guys have room for one more?"

"You better have some skills, boy," a man with grey hair and a grey beard says. "I'll put you on my team." He hands a cue to Bogdan.

"I'll try not to disappoint you," Bogdan says. "I'm Vlad. Nice to meet you." He holds his hand out for a handshake.

"I'm Dmytro. Now let's kick their asses." The rest of the crew laughs in response.

Bogdan is a bit surprised that everyone is so friendly there. It should be one of the darkest places in Kiev.

The game progresses until only a few balls are left.

"It's up to you, Vlad," Dmytro says. "Put that yellow one in the hole, and then there'll only be the black one left."

Feeling the pressure, Bogdan concentrates on the ball, taking nearly thirty seconds to aim. When he pulls the cue stick back to shoot, something strikes the back of his head.

Dmytro swings a baseball bat one more time and hits Bogdan again in the back of his head. More people stand up and start hitting Bogdan with their fists. They hit him in his face, stomach, and back until he falls, unconscious.

"Throw him off the bridge," Dmytro says, "with a rock tied to his leg."

A couple of other guys lift Bogdan and carry him outside the pub. It's dark, and the people who notice something is wrong just turn and look away. They're used to seeing all kinds of shit close to this pub.

The bridge is just a few meters away. The guys lift Bogdan up and wait as one of the guys ties one end of a rope to his leg and the other end to a rock. Then they throw him over the fence. After a big splash, the surface is flat again as Bogdan's body sinks immediately.

CHAPTER 11

Let's Go To Paris

Alice and David are sitting on the balcony in their big house in a small town called Alice Springs in Australia. She was born there, which was why her parents named her "Alice." She has always loved that place even though, after traveling half of the world, she realizes her little town doesn't have much to offer.

The trip to Bali took place just a few days ago. After she dealt with Cheslav and his gang, she spent a day and a half taking some pictures and videos for Instagram. She doesn't want anyone to doubt anything, especially David.

"Urgh, seeing your pictures from Bali reminds me of how much I need a vacation," David says while wrapping his arms around her.

"Well, you can take a week off, and we can fly some-where," Alice suggests while sipping her wine.

The weather is beautiful. Their timber-frame balcony faces the sunset. It's like a movie. Every day at around 6:00 p.m., they sip wine and wait for the same postcard image. The sun is going to take a rest, and the moon will take over the watch.

"Maybe we should do that!" David says, confidence in his voice.

"Oh? Sure, where do you wanna go?" She's surprised by his agreement, but she currently has no missions, so why not?

"Let's go to Paris!" David says while looking at his glass of red wine, which gave him the idea. "What do you think?"

"It's too classy for me, but all right, let's do it." She raises her glass to David, and they clink them together to confirm their plans.

"I'll open another bottle to celebrate!" David says, waving his empty glass and picking up the empty bottle on his way to the living room. "Paris, baby!"

Alice is sitting by herself watching the sunset and thinking about "that guy" again. She's upset. It was five years ago, and now she's with David, so why do her thoughts fly to the other guy every time she's by herself?

Alice rubs her face with her hands to refresh her thoughts and then reaches for her bag on the small table next to her, but then she remembers she left the bag in the living room. She wants to get her phone and play some music. Alice notices David's phone on the table and reaches for it. She really wants some music.

Alice tries to unlock his phone with the usual "A" pattern as a symbol for her name, but it doesn't work. She's confused. Yesterday she used his phone to see some old pictures, and it worked.

She tries again and nothing. *Is he cheating on me?* She wonders. But she's so sure of his love that it doesn't make any sense. Then it occurs to her. It can't be. Is he with the Nobodies too? It's a crazy thought, but her instincts tell her that nothing is impossible.

She's ready to try the pattern to unlock one more time, but this time, with the letter "N." She hesitates for a moment and then does it quickly as if removing a Band-Aid.

Impossible. It unlocks!

She notices that he also has the Nobodies application on his phone. What does this mean?

"Sorry to keep you waiting, sugar," David says as he returns with two glasses of wine. "I was searching for this beautiful bottle of red wine from Bordeaux. Let's have a little taste of France before the trip, shall we?" He sounds even more excited than before as he holds out a glass.

"Oh, but my love, you know I don't like to mix drinks," she says. "I already had two glasses of white wine." That's true, but she also doesn't know what to think. Maybe he's trying to poison her. *But it can't be,* she thinks. *What if I'm just overreacting?*

"When it comes to this Cabernet Sauvignon, it's worth dying for!" David says.

She accepts the glass and then reaches for his as well, placing them on the wooden table next to them. "OK, if you say so, it must be worth it. You've always had good taste in wine, plus I already feel drunk, so it shouldn't make any difference" Alice approaches him, putting her left hand on his man area and starts rubbing while softly biting his bottom lip. She can feel his dick getting harder, and she moves down from his bottom lip to his neck.

David tilts his head back, allowing her better access to his neck.

Suddenly, Alice breaks the moment and raises her glass. "To Paris!"

David looks at her for a moment and then grabs his glass "To Paris!"

They look at each other for a second as if wondering who will sip first. Then Alice takes a couple of sips, and David does the same. Then she closes her eyes. "Oh my God, you're right, this wine is delicious!"

David nods. "It's an excellent wine. I told you." He takes another sip and then sets his glass on the table.

"So, when are we going to Paris?" she asks, excited and a bit drunk.

"Alice, darling, we're not going to Paris," he says as she looks at him with her big blue eyes. "You're just a mission."

"A mission?" she asks, frowning in confusion.

"I know what you do, and I know you're using my Vitolicerin 12," David says. "Basically, we're together because that's what I was instructed to do up to this moment. I would make supplies for you and pretend I didn't know you were taking it. That was my part; you're the weapon."

"Hmm . . . why this moment?" Alice asks, revealing her cards as well. "What's changed?"

David shrugs. "It's simply a matter of following orders. We don't get the reason. As a matter of fact, we don't ask anything, do we? We get the mission, and we execute it, or we become the next mission, and we're executed. Don't get me wrong; I did enjoy my time with you. But it's you or me. It's as simple as that."

"I'm glad you understand how the game works," Alice replies.

David shakes his head slowly. "Alice, you don't understand. I'm saying all of this because you're dying."

"Oh, that's too bad," Alice says. "Then I guess we're really not going to Paris." She pretends to be disappointed.

"This isn't a joke, Alice, I put the Vit—"

"Vitolicerin 12 in my wine?" Alice asks. She opens her eyes even wider. "Don't bother. It just makes the wine taste better."

"I don't know if you're drunk or what, but I guess it doesn't matter," David said. "I just wanted to say those things before your time is up."

"You know, you're a good scientist, David, and a good teacher. It's been a pleasure knowing you." She sits on her chair and places her right hand on her chest as David watches her.

"Just relax," he says. "Don't resist it, and it will be over soon." He turns around and walks away slowly.

"It starts with chest pain and coughing, right?" she asks.

David stops for a moment without saying anything.

"I wasn't joking," Alice said. "You're a good teacher."

David starts panting and falls to his knees. Alice stands up and walks toward him with a glass of wine in her hand. "You hear this sound?" She shakes the glass, and it sounds like a small piece of metal is rattling around inside.

"This can't be!" David exclaims. "How did you know?" He starts coughing while looking at Alice's right hand. She's wiggling her fingers like she wants to point something out.

"Vitolicerin 12 is the deadliest poison in the world, but if it comes in contact with Rhodium, it becomes less harmful than a glass of Coca-Cola. Those are your words, remember?" She places the glass close to his face, and he notices the engagement ring that he gave her, made of Rhodium, on the bottom of the glass.

"But . . . but I didn't put any in my glass, and I poured both glasses . . ." He coughs more and more, fighting for breath, then falls to the ground.

"I guess you were enjoying those kisses on the neck too much," Alice says. "I placed more than enough Vitolicerin 12 to kill an elephant in yours, but it seems like you were thinking with a different head at that moment."

"Urgh . . . You . . . Bitch . . ." He begins to foam at the mouth, and then his body seizes up, and he dies in tremendous pain a few seconds after.

She takes her ring out of the glass and places it back on her finger, then sits comfortably in her balcony chair. Sunset is almost finished.

"I guess Paris isn't a bad idea after all."

CHAPTER 12

Do You Think We Changed The World?

"So, I see you decided to start your little project without our approval," Vera says. "That's just like you, Connor, selfish and arrogant." They are sitting on a bench close to the water somewhere in Switzerland. It's only two of them this time, without Gamba and Pierre.

"You know better than anyone that it's necessary," Connor replies calmly while looking at the blue water in front of them.

"Maybe, but it's about respect. You're getting worse with age, you know."

"Respect isn't just a word, even though many people believe that, you know. Hey, Vera, you know what? I respect you! Easy, right? I trust and respect you guys more than I trust and respect myself. A couple of decades working with me should have proved that."

"A couple of decades working with you has taught us that you're very stubborn," Vera replies. They both chuckle for a moment. "We also know that if you're doing something that seems, well, evil, like killing the majority of our Nobodies, you have an idea behind it that's justifying such an awful act and brings greater good to the world."

Connor shrugs. "Maybe. Tell me, do you think we changed the world?"

"Well, I know we made some hard decisions," Vera replies. "Probably the hardest decisions that anyone has ever made, and we will keep doing that, so if you think that having too many Nobodies can affect our committee and the blood and sweat that we invested for so long, then we're with you all the way, whatever it takes."

Connor shakes his head. "That's not what I meant. I meant, did we really change the world with our actions? Have we made the world a better place? I feel like we haven't."

"Why do you think like that all of a sudden?"

"I feel that we've been failing in what we're doing for many years now."

"Now you're being too hard on yourself," Vera says. "Please don't make me remind you how much you care about this organization and how far you'll go to protect it!"

Connor shakes his head and then stands up. "This world doesn't need protection. This world needs a villain." With that, he turns and walks away as Vera watches him go in silence.

CHAPTER 13

A Quiet Night In Istanbul

Onur Aga, the Nobody from Turkey, is walking home from the grocery store.

The streets of Istanbul are so beautiful at night. It isn't busy; in fact, almost no one is on the streets at all.

He sees a beautiful black girl walking toward him and texting on her phone. *She's hot*, he thinks while waiting to see if she will make eye contact with him.

She finishes texting and then puts her phone in the brown purse that's over her shoulder.

Onur Aga is happy when she not only makes eye contact but also offers him a little smile as well.

He opens his mouth to say "Hello," but manages only to say "He . . ." when he sees a spark coming through her purse and feels the bullets from her silenced gun stabbing him in his chest, leaving him speechless and in shock.

He falls to his knees, then falls forward and dies with his eyes wide open, as if searching for an answer that he will never find.

Nala passes by him, acting like nothing happened. There is no noise, no drama, just one less Nobody to kill.

CHAPTER 14

The Intruder

"Have a good night, Lieutenant. I hope I won't see you when I come back in the morning!" Brigadier Blanc announces as the elevator doors close.

Lieutenant Liam Mercier merely nods, too focused on the paper in front of him to reply.

No one is left in the police station except him, two security guards, and an overnight operator, all of them on the ground floor.

Liam's office is on the first floor. The only light comes from his desk lamp, so he can read. As he reads, his mind wanders .

So I start digging deeper, asking questions, and suddenly there's a guy trying to kill me? I don't need proof bigger than that. I'm definitely getting close to something or someone. What bothers me is that the guy who attacked me had no police record. Jeff Peterson, forty-three years old, wife and two kids—twins, a boy and a girl. Worked in a coffee factory in Dublin . . . Ireland? What the hell was he doing in Paris? Liam is getting more excited by the second. Even though he hasn't slept more than three hours since the attack—he has been in the office basically twenty hours a day—the thrill of solving this case makes him numb to tiredness.

Liam is a good cop. He started at the bottom and within a few years became a lieutenant. He has a winning attitude and the power of will to become the best in his field, and people around him know it will happen eventually. Criminals in France don't like him at all.

Liam is thirty-four years old, smart, brave, good looking, and extremely skillful when it comes to weapons. The ladies love him. He looks like Edward Norton, the actor—tall, short brown hair, handsome smile, and stylish beard.

Feeling like he could use a coffee and a two-minute break, Liam stands up, opens his eyes and mouth wide to stretch his face muscles, and automatically starts yawning.

As he does, the elevator doors open, revealing a person in a ski mask and a long black coat. Immediately, the person starts shooting at him with a silenced pistol!

Before Liam can throw himself behind his desk, he's hit in his left leg and his left arm.

Crouching behind his desk, he grabs his Glock, which is hanging on his gun belt over his chair, and returns fire in the direction where he saw the intruder without raising his head over his desk.

He doesn't hear any return shots, so he peeks over his desk. He can't see or hear anyone.

Liam knows there is no way that an intruder who shot him two times will run away. He just wants Liam to think he's gone. Liam looks at the holes in his arm and leg and realizes they're bleeding intensely.

He's waiting for me to make a move, or he knows I'll bleed out! Liam is nervous, but he manages to stay focused enough to make a plan.

There are supposed to be a few policemen on the ground floor. Did he kill them?

Liam lies on the floor and looks through a small space between the floor and the front panel of his desk. He sees the only door behind which he thinks the intruder is hiding. However, he will only be able to see the intruder's feet if he shows himself.

He decides to pretend to call the cops. "Hello, yes, 911? I have an emergency. Please help me. There's an intruder in the . . ." Before he finishes the sentence, he sees black shoes and fires three shots, two of which possibly hit the intruder's foot before he runs away. *Elegant shoes?* Liam is confused because the guy appears to be a pro hitman. He expected black boots, at least.

He doesn't know if he should chase the guy because he's wounded as well, but adrenaline is pumping strong now, and he stands up and creeps toward the doors where he last saw the intruder, his Glock pointed in front of him. Liam is ready to shoot at the slightest movement.

While Liam passes through the doorframe, the intruder manages to snatch Liam's Glock out of his hands while raising his gun toward Liam. Liam grabs his hands, and he and the intruder begin wrestling for the intruder's gun.

With all his strength, Liam steps on the intruder's wounded foot. In the blink of an eye, the intruder presses the magazine release, and the magazine falls out from the gun.

One bullet is left in the chamber, and Liam points it at the intruder.

"Remove the mask," Liam says. The intruder doesn't move. "I said remove the mask, or I'll remove it from your corpse!" Liam is angry, and adrenaline is coursing through his body.

He can kill the intruder in this situation, but he wants to capture him and ask him questions that will be crucial to the mystery of why people are trying to assassinate him.

The intruder slowly raises his hands toward the back of his ski mask. Unbeknownst to Liam, the intruder presses a button on his watch when both hands are hidden behind his head.

Liam feels a jolt of electricity in his left leg and left arm where he got shot by the intruder. The bullets are still inside Liam. It turns out they are some high-tech bullets.

At that moment, as a reaction to being shocked, Liam fires the last bullet, which passes close enough intruder's ear to cause a flesh wound. The intruder seizes the moment to run away because it's not worth fighting for the pistol magazine, which is closer to Liam.

Liam recovers quickly and looks around. He finds the magazine and puts it back in the gun. He thinks about using the stairs to get help, but he knows that with his wounds, he can't move very fast.

He goes to the window and sees the intruder getting in a black car parked just outside the station. He doesn't think it's worth shooting the car from where he is. Then the intruder gets out of the car carrying something that looks like an AK-47 and rushes back into the police station.

Liam just stands and stares. He has never been more afraid for his life.

CHAPTER 15

Best Friends

Leo growls. Victor opens his eyes and for the first few seconds tries to understand where is he and what's happening.

It's morning, and he and Leo are surrounded by people.

Victor tries to sit up by putting weight on his left hand, and the sharp pain he feels causes a flashback of the events from a few hours earlier.

"Sir, are you alright? What happened here?" One of the people from the crowd approaches him.

Victor shakes his head slowly in confusion. "I'm not sure. Wait . . . Lucy! Hey, have you seen my wife? Short black hair, dark eyes?" He stands up quickly and feels a bit dizzy.

"Uh, no, actually. We were just hiking here when we saw you and your dog and these two dead wolves and blood everywhere. Both of you need to see a doctor ASAP!"

"Where the hell is she?" Victor asks, turning his head slowly as he scans the woods. "Something isn't right," he adds quietly to himself while crouching next to Leo, who is lying next to him, awake.

He inspects Leo's body for wounds and notices how the blood on him has become dry and smelly. There are lots of bite marks, but his life doesn't appear to be in danger.

"Was it only these two wolves or were there more?" the guy asks.

Victor starts having flashbacks and feels a headache coming on. "There were more of them. I'm only alive because of this brave guy." He kisses the top of Leo's head.

The police and an ambulance show up in response to a call from the hikers. They take Victor and Leo in the ambulance.

Throughout the trip, Victor tries to figure out what happened the night before. *Lucy left to pee behind the trees. A moment later, wolves showed up. There was no scream from Lucy, nothing, I don't think they attacked her. So how did she vanish? And what the hell happened?*

This must be the response from The Nobodies. That was a stupid move to say I was coming for them. If not yesterday, they'll try again today or tomorrow and the day after until they put me down for good.

The doctors treat his wounds, and he gets a few stitches on his left hand as well as a couple for the cuts on his legs and back that he doesn't even remember getting.

The small veterinary team across the street takes care of Leo as well. They clean his wounds and stitch him up here and there. They also put a big cone on his neck, so he can't reach the stitches and rip them out. He has trouble putting his weight on his right-rear leg because some ligaments were destroyed by the wolf's strong bite.

"Excuse me, Mr. Volta" one of the veterinarians says. "While stitching up your dog, we found this. It looks like a chip or a micro SD card that was inserted under his skin. Do you know anything about that?"

Victor examines it. "Uh, isn't it a dog microchip? You know, if he gets lost or something?"

The doctor shakes his head. "No, that's still under his skin. We found that as well." He pauses and looks at Victor. "Are you sure you're able to drive home to Vancouver?" Victor gives the doctor a thumbs-up and then hobbles out the door, Leo at his side.

As Victor waits to be released, he tries to sort out what happened, but he's interrupted when a policeman comes to take his statement and assure him once again that they swept the woods and never found any trace of his wife, which Victor assumes is a good sign, meaning she's still alive.

Then another thought occurs to him. Did The Nobodies kidnap her and lead the wolves to him and Leo? Definitely a possibility. Of course, Victor doesn't mention that to the police officer. Other officers are searching for the rest of the wolves, so there are no other suspects in this situation.

The policeman and the doctors praise Leo for his bravery, mentioning to Victor how lucky they both are.

Victor and Leo limp out of the hospital together, two best friends who survived a horrible night standing up for each other, but Victor knows more horrible nights and days are about to come. He needs to find Lucy before The Nobodies do—if they don't have her already.

CHAPTER 16

What. A. Shot.

"That was a good game, mate," Marlon says, praising his friend Thomas after a tennis game. "Your forehand is really something!"

"Well, I told you, the easiest way to lose fifty dollars is to bet you'll win against me, but you didn't listen!"

"One more set left," Marlon says. "You're getting tired, so I have a chance!"

Thomas is one of the Nobodies. Originally from Australia, he came to England when he was quite young and has spent most of his life there. He plays tennis in a semi-pro league, which serves to cover his actual work as a Nobody.

"OK, if you say so!" Thomas wipes the sweat from his face with a small white towel and gets back on the court.

"Give me your best serve!" Marlon says. He isn't very good at tennis, but he's very optimistic.

"Here comes the sniper!" Thomas throws the tennis ball high in the air when, ironically enough, a bullet from a sniper splits his head in half.

It's impossible to tell what hits the ground first—Thomas's body, the tennis ball, or his racket—but it's safe to say that Marlon will have nightmares until the end of his life.

At least, he won the match though . . .

CHAPTER 17

"D" Unexpected Gift

Bogdan feels like somebody is rapidly slapping him on his left cheek and he slowly opens his eyes. He realizes he's naked but covered with a blanket.

"I needed to remove your clothes because they were soaked," a man says. "How are you feeling?" The man has long black hair that matches his long black beard. He's sitting in front of Bogdan.

"I feel like everything is moving," Bogdan says, looking around.

"That's because you're on a fishing boat, son. You can tell by the smell."

Bogdan raises his head, and his nostrils flare. He tries to stand up but feels pain all over his body—in his muscles, bones, head . . .

"I cleaned most of your wounds," the fisherman says. "You'll have plenty of bruises and will feel pain over the next few days or so, but apart from that, you'll be alright. Was it a bar fight? These things are very common here, but Kiev isn't always like this."

"Wait," Bogdan says. "Did you jump in the water to save me? You don't even know who I am." Bogdan eyes him suspiciously.

"Son, not everyone here in Kiev is a bad person. I spend my days and nights on this boat. I don't mind getting a little wet from time to time."

"Sorry," Bogdan says. "Life has taught me not to trust to anyone, not even to people who try to help me. I'm really thankful. You saved my life. There must be something that I can help you with. I can't just leave."

"I've been living like this for most of my life. Whatever I catch in these waters I sell, and it's enough to make a living. Kiev isn't expensive, not when you live on a fishing boat. Although there might be one thing you can do for me . . ." His eyes narrow, and he starts biting his nails. Then he stands up and opens the cabin door.

"Anything!" Bogdan says, excited he can return the favor, at least partially.

A dog comes through the door, and Bogdan doesn't know what to say. It has a black face and ears, a black chest, black legs, and black fur under its tail, but it's quite the opposite on top of its body. Its neck, back, and the upper side of its tail are light yellow. It looks like the dog jumped in black paint but didn't quite sink. It's beautiful.

"One of my friends who knows dog breeds better than I do said she's a Belgian Malinois," the fisherman says. "He said she might be one year old." He switches on a flashlight and points it at her.

"I mean . . . I can't really . . . I don't . . ." Bogdan is caught completely off guard.

"I pulled her out of this river just like I did with you. She was trapped in an old fishing net next to the docks. That was just three days ago, so she's still not very attached to me.

I figure I spend so much time on this boat, and she requires a lot of exercise and running. Like my friend said, they use these dogs in the police now. She's becoming anxious on the boat. I'm not much of a land person, and I didn't really save her from drowning if I give her a life that will make her miserable. I want you to take her. You look like someone who exercises, someone who can give her the kind of life she deserves."

"Maybe I can do something else," Bogdan says, his eyes on the dog. "Maybe . . . I mean . . . what's her name?" She keeps staring at him as if she's trying to hypnotize him. He starts to like the idea of not being constantly alone.

"I named her Dnieper," the fisherman says. "That's the name of this river, but I call her 'D' for short. You can call her whatever you want." He's a little sad to give her away. He loves her company on the boat, but he can tell that she isn't entirely happy to spend her days and nights on the boat. He's a good man.

Bogdan nods as he scratches her behind the ears. "Dnieper . . . I like that name."

CHAPTER 18

What Now?

Paris is a bit colder than Alice expected and a bit less glamorous, just a lot of drunk people roaming the streets and taking selfies and group pictures even though it's already past midnight. Alice had expected more from Paris, or maybe she's just feeling lonely. She drives slowly back to her hotel. She needs time to think about everything.

It has been more than a week since the incident with David. When Alice poisoned him, she thought should she try to make it look like a suicide, but she was aware that it would be almost impossible to do. Their house is quite a distance from other houses in the area, and she figured the best thing to do was to bury him somewhere in the desert and then report him as missing.

It took lots of time to put him in the car. At one point she almost gave up because his body was so heavy. After a struggle, she got him in the trunk and then drove for nearly 100 km into the desert. She was terrified. After she dug a hole and buried David's body, she returned home.

Her face was blank. She was paler than usual, and her mind was working constantly on how to get away from everything. She didn't have time to cry or panic because, on one side, she needed to have a perfect story for the police, and on the other side, she knew she was being haunted by The Nobodies. It looked like a dead end.

She cleaned the house, disposed of the wine glasses and bottles, and returned everything to normal. Then the next morning, she went to his laboratory.

Alice stormed into the building without saying anything and rushed straight to his laboratory.

Security knew her because she'd come often to visit David, and she would never check in because she was Mrs. Hill, the boss's wife. "It's a lunch break, Mrs. Hill," the security guard said. "Probably no one is in the laboratory . . ."

The elevator door closed before he could finish, and she was on her way to the laboratory. She knew the laboratory would be unattended during lunch.

She entered the huge white room and went straight to where the Vitolicerin 12 was kept, looking around casually to make sure no one was watching.

She pulled an empty Gatorade bottle from her bag and transferred the purple liquid into it. Then she placed the bottle back in her bag and rushed back to the security desk in the lobby.

"I want you to call my husband to come here immediately!" she said. With her eyes open wide and her finger pointed at the phone, she scared the shit out of the security guard, who wasn't sure if he should disturb Mr. Hill on his break, but Mr. Hill had always told his employees to respect her the way they respected him.

Eventually, Alice played them all. She convinced them that she didn't have any idea why David wasn't at work, and she came to search for him because she suspected he had a mistress. She said he left the previous night, saying he couldn't do it anymore, that Alice travels so much that sometimes he felt like he didn't even have a wife. He didn't return, so she assumed he had gone directly to work. Alice spiced up the situation with some good old crying, playing the part of a wife who had been cheated on and abandoned.

The police promised to search for him if he did not show up in the evening, but they thought it was nothing more than a little trouble in paradise between two married people.

After a few days when David failed to show up at work or at home, as dead people are wont to do, they took the situation more seriously. But after questioning her alibi and intentions, nobody suspected Alice, and everyone tried to give her support and promised they would find David.

She sure hopes they never do.

CHAPTER 19

A Bullet For Him

Victor can hear Leo's loud bark, but it takes time for him to figure out if it's really happening or if he's dreaming.

He straightens himself up in bed and sees Leo standing in front of the bedroom door, though the barking has stopped.

Looking out the window, Victor realizes it's morning, and he has probably slept for over twelve hours. His pain seems to have doubled now that the adrenaline is completely gone. Leo comes and gives him a quick lick on the cheek, as if in sympathy.

After going to the washroom and going through his morning routine, Victor's stomach growls. He's starving.

When he walks into the kitchen, he notices an envelope on the dining table. He tries to remember if it was there the night before or if someone just put it there, which would explain why Leo was barking.

He picks up the envelope, which is blank, then rips it open and pulls out the letter.

> Mr. Volta, we're glad that you're well. We've had some issues with each other recently, but we are ready to welcome you back to the team! We are men of our word, and it will be done as it says, and you'll not need to look over your shoulder anymore.

Oh, by the way, your wife is unharmed!

We do require a small gesture of loyalty from your side though, as you can understand. Pick up the gun that you're hiding under your bed, and kill your dog. We will come to pick up his body. You have until noon to decide which body we will come to pick up

Victor stands there for a moment, thinking. Then he goes to his bedroom, kneels down beside his bed, and reaches under it for the pistol he has hidden there.

"Come on, Leo," he says, standing up. "Let's go to the garage."

Leo is excited and wags his small docked tail.

The garage door opens, and for the first time, Victor allows Leo in. Leo has never done that before. When the door closes, not a sound is heard outside because the garage is soundproof.

After approximately half an hour, Victor comes out carrying a bloodstained cream blanket wrapped around something and places it in his backyard.

He knows they are watching, and they mentioned they would come to pick up the body. He goes back into the garage.

It's a beautiful sunny day. Birds are singing, the sky is clear, and it's neither too cold nor not too warm. Just perfect.

A "mailman" parks in the driveway and then gets out and walks toward the front door of Victor's house, slowly scanning everything around him.

He notices a bloody blanket on the back side of the house. Victor made it barely noticeable but still visible for anyone who was looking for it.

The mailman approaches the blanket and then crouches next to it and unwraps it. His eyes go wide when he realizes the bloody blanket doesn't contain a dead dog but a car tire cut in half. A note is attached to the tire. It contains only two words: "Look Up!"

The man starts shaking and breathing heavily, knowing what's coming, but before he can think any further, the bullet fired by Victor from the top of the roof goes through his forehead, and he falls over, dead.

Victor drags him inside and throws him in the same hole where he put Mr. Wilson a couple of weeks earlier.

He's already packed, and Leo is waiting in the car. The garage door opens, and before coming out, he turns on the radio, blasting "Turn the Page" by Bob Seger.

"Let's go find Mom," Victor says, petting Leo's head. "What do you say, boy?" Leo just looks at Victor as he smiles and presses the gas pedal.

CHAPTER 20

Drive!

"This guy is insane!" Liam says as he looks at how many bullets he has left in the magazine. He thinks about calling 911 for real this time, but he can already hear footsteps below as the intruder rushes back up the stairs. Liam noticed that the intruder was surprisingly quick, even though the bullet flew through his foot earlier. *Maybe was just a scratch? This guy is not leaving until he finishes the job*, Liam was thinking.

Liam looks around the room, searching for a bigger gun or anything else that might help him. Nothing, just a few empty desks. All the guns are on the ground floor.

"There's no way I'm winning this with the pistol, not against this guy."

Liam looks out the window and notices a small truck with a tall trailer parked below. He knows exactly what he needs to do. He whips the window open.

The moment he lands on the trailer, he rolls forward to reduce the pressure on his spine, but he rolls a bit too far and falls on the hood of a passing car, cracking the windshield as well.

"What the hell?" Alice, the driver, cranks the wheel and then slams on the brakes, which makes Liam fall to the ground. Liam stands up as quickly as his body will allow and opens the passenger door, then jumps inside.

"Drive! Drive fast if you want to live!" he yells, pointing the gun at her.

"OK, OK, I'm driving!" She barely finishes the sentence when bullets fly through the car's roof, one of them passing straight through Alice's left thigh. She screams but manages to press the gas pedal. "What's happening?" She's angry, fearful, and confused as bullets continue flying through and around the car.

"Just drive. Turn left here. I'll take the wheel. You can't drive with that leg!"

"Who are you!? And why the fuck did you have to fall on my car of all the fucking cars in Paris!?" She's furious, tears sliding down her cheeks as her big blue eyes almost pop out of her head.

Liam remains calm as they exchange seats once they round a corner, so the intruder can't reach them.

He drives fast, assuming the intruder will get into his car and follow them, but Liam knows the city well, and in no time he's heading for the nearest hospital, so they can have their wounds treated.

While driving, he explains to Alice that he's a lieutenant in the French police force and briefly tells her about the lunatic who attacked him.

Once they reach the hospital, they are taken to different rooms. Liam feels weird lying on the bed while doctors rush around him. He has just been attacked and shot, jumped out a window, and was hit by the car, and yet the only thing he can think about is how damn beautiful Alice is.

CHAPTER 21

This Planet's Biggest Enemy

"Didn't we meet just a few weeks ago?" Gamba asks as he takes a seat and looks at other members of the committee for an answer. "It isn't easy to get away from Chidike that often without her wondering something. She's a smart woman, you know." Chidike is his wife. Gamba is one of the most dangerous people in the world, but he's not number one in his marriage. Chidike is a lioness.

"I agree," Pierre says. "What's happening?" Of course, all eyes are on Connor.

"As you already know," Connor says, "the project of eliminating Nobodies is happening right now."

"Many of them have been successfully eliminated, as you planned," Vera says. As usual, her eyes narrow as she focuses on the topic at hand.

Connor nods. "Indeed. However, I wasn't completely honest last time. I haven't shared with you the real reason why I wanted to start this project."

His comments are met by silence. The room they are in looks like an ordinary living room. It is in one of the many houses that The Nobodies own for the purpose of such secret meetings.

"I sent Nobodies to kill each other," Connor says. "In particular, I sent the ones that we considered the better ones to kill the lesser ones, but the purpose was to find the best ten Nobodies who can perfectly execute the big project that I've been planning for years." Everyone is looking and listening carefully now.

"I would like to remind you of a few things," Connor continues. "When the My Life social networking website first showed up and became popular, we knew it would be bad for humanity in the long term, so we eliminated the founder and destroyed the company.

"Now we have Facebook and a million other social networking websites, so I would say we failed because we can't kill everyone who comes up with a new idea for social networking. That's not how we do things.

"We have also prevented war between Russian and the USA maybe twenty times so far, but still, it's just a matter of time.

"We've eliminated every person who has brought anything new that's bad into the world. The newspapers claim that many famous people have died by accident, but we know what really happened, where it happened, and why.

"Drug dealers continue to proliferate no matter how many we eliminate. They grow like grass. The same is true of poachers and serial killers, and don't even get me started with politicians."

"Sounds like we did all those things for nothing," Vera says as she sips vodka from a small glass that she poured while Connor was talking.

"It wasn't for nothing," Connor says. "It was meant to be to show us that we need to change the way we do things."

"What sort of change are you talking about?" Pierre asks, intrigued to learn more.

"The point is, we did all of that for the well-being of this planet," Connor says. "We assumed most people are basically good, but we've learned that isn't true. People have become selfish, so selfish that nature, animals, and other people who do care are suffering. There are too many of them. It has to stop.

"Alcohol and drugs take millions of lives yearly, but the wrong lives. People who consume these things often kill someone else before they kill themselves.

"Cigarettes demonstrate clearly that people don't care for their own health, which makes me wonder why we should. Who cares that it's terrible for nature, animals, other people, and the entire planet? It's important that I feel good while I smoke, right? That's the mentality.

"Look at the animals. They just want to be left alone to live their lives, but poachers prefer money for their body parts, the zoos prefer money for their imprisoned lives, and we cut forests and jungles to build more cities and factories to make more money.

"Everyone thinks they're so important, more important than nature, animals, and the person standing next to them. Tell me, what have humans become?" He eyes them all, but they are waiting for him to answer. "I'll tell you," he continues. "Selfish villains. We, humans, we are this planet's biggest enemy."

Vera, Gamba, and Pierre have never been more confused. Nor have they ever seen Connor so upset.

He sits back in his chair and slides his fingers through his gray hair, making it neat again.

"Well, what do you suggest?" Vera finally asks. She's not sure if she wants to know the answer.

"I think people on this planet need some discipline," he replies confidently.

Pierre shakes his head in confusion. "I'm not sure what you're suggesting."

"Are you saying we need to destroy human life on this planet?" Gamba asks.

Connor leans forward, meeting their gazes in turn. "I'm saying that if the four of us don't do something about it, no one else will."

CHAPTER 22

The Young Protector

Many years ago, somewhere in Europe

"What happened, my son?" Darya asks. "Did you get in another fight?" Darya is Igor's mom. She just opened the front door and found him with his nose bleeding and his face covered in mud.

"They killed the ants," Igor says, anger in his voice and tears in his eyes. Igor is eight years old.

Darya frowns. "The ants?"

"They were just living their lives and carrying some crumbs around their small houses, and then these mean kids started stepping on them. Why would they do that? We're so much bigger than them. It's not fair!" He starts crying and hugs his mom.

This is not the first time such a thing has happened. Igor flipped when his teacher killed a bee with a notebook. He threw a rock at a kid who kicked a small dog that the other kids were playing with. He bit another kid's hand because the kid was pulling a cat's tail. He always wants to fight the bullies at school when they abuse other kids and often comes home with bruises and cuts.

Some other kids might be bothered by such things, but Igor becomes so protective when things aren't fair for someone that he will fight while other kids might just say, "Oh, that's too bad" or "Poor thing."

At age fifteen, he realizes he isn't strong enough or big enough to deal with all the problems around, so he saves his lunch money and uses it to pay older boys to help him with certain issues. For example, one time Thomas, Igor's best friend, went on his first date when one of the school bullies approached him to make fun of him. But the older kid who Igor gave money grabbed him by the ear and asked him to apologize to Thomas, making Thomas look cool in front of the girl.

When Igor is twenty, Thomas is hit by a car driven by a drunk driver and dies on the spot. The next day Igor stabs the driver to death and then runs away.

Later, everything is a mystery. He changes his name to Connor and climbs to one of the highest branches in the world, creating his own company, which he uses to pay the good guys to deal with the bad guys, just like he did when he was a kid, only now the entire planet is his playground.

CHAPTER 23

A Day On The Beach

One month after the attempt on Bogdan's life

"Come on, D, you can do it!" He throws a red Frisbee and encourages Dnieper to catch it before it falls to the ground. "Yes! Good girl!" Bogdan yells when D catches the Frisbee and runs back to him.

Bogdan is wearing a blue baseball hat, a red shirt, and grey sweatpants, quite the opposite of his favorite all-black style.

For the past month, Bogdan has been in the United States. After the incident in Kiev, he's pretty sure that something suspicious is happening and that The Nobodies want him dead.

No missions have come through for the past month, and considering circumstances, Bogdan decided it was best to move to another continent for a bit.

He bought a camper and has been on the road since then. He knows staying in hotels will be dangerous because it's one of the easiest ways to find someone. It's working so far. It's been a month, and he still hasn't encountered any situations that would put him in danger.

It's been a month of training for him and D . Bogdan has never been in better shape, and he has also managed to teach D multiple tricks by watching how-to videos on YouTube.

D is gorgeous! She can do anything: climb a tree, climb a wall, swim, jump high, and run super-fast. Bogdan falls in love with her instantly, realizing that the old fisherman was right that she needs a lot of exercise. He can understand why the police use this breed.

D drops the Frisbee at Bogdan's feet. She's ready for more! They are in one of San Francisco's biggest and most popular parks, Fort Funstone. It's a huge park with an area next to the sea and a huge beach that's usually empty because most dog owners prefer the grassy upper area, which is way warmer and does not have the freezing breeze that always finds a way to sneak under people's clothes and make them shiver.

The silence is precious for Bogdan. He's had a hard time finding a good, silent place. The beach is it. He can only hear the waves and the wind and occasionally D barking when Bogdan gets lost in thought and forgets to throw the Frisbee for a few seconds. The cold doesn't bother him; he's from Russia, after all.

D picks up the Frisbee and lifts her head, standing in one place looking in the distance. Curious, Bogdan looks in the same direction. He sees a man and a dog on the beach playing together in the distance. Suddenly, D runs toward them, which confuses Bogdan because she's usually focused on the Frisbee and him and not very interested in other people or dogs.

"D! Come here, girl, let's play!" He picks up the Frisbee, but she doesn't listen and keeps running toward the guy and his dog. Bogdan runs after her, thinking that something is going on. He quickly checks his gun, which is hidden under his shirt, and presses it to his body to make sure it doesn't fall out of his holster as he runs.

The guy and the dog notice that D and Bogdan are running toward them, but the man doesn't react. D isn't running at full speed, and Bogdan is pretty close to her, and then both of them are close to the other guy and his dog.

Bogdan notices the other dog take a few steps forward in front of his owner. Now he's close enough to see that the dog is quite big and muscular. It's a black dog, and he remembers the breed from all the YouTube videos that he watched while training D. Before he can think of anything else, the black dog grabs D by the neck and with one strong judo-like move, throws her to the ground!

Bogdan almost pulls his gun out until he notices that after the black dog throws D to the ground, he doesn't attack any further. Instead, he walks back and stands tall in front of his owner.

D returns to Bogdan, and he checks her neck. There's no blood or scratches. It was just a protection move to throw her off her feet.

"I'm very sorry," the owner of the black dog says. "He just thought she might attack me because she was running so fast toward us. I hope she's OK." He speaks with a calm tone, and his face has a cold look, almost like he doesn't mean it.

"She's fine," Bogdan says. "Just a year old and full of energy. I can understand your dog's perspective. My dog needs to learn not to rush toward other dogs." D lies down next to Bogdan, focused on the black dog.

"She isn't afraid," the owner of the black dog says while studying D. "Her posture indicates she's quite relaxed. She can read good energy from my dog."

"He's a Doberman, right?" Bogdan says. He knows the answer, but the number of scars on the black dog are scary. Some are on his face, some on the legs, and he has one big one on his stomach. It looks like he has been through a serious fight or accident. Bogdan wants to ask, but it's a sensitive topic, so he doesn't.

"Yes," the man says. "His name is Leo."

CHAPTER 24

The Best Perfume In The World

"I miss Paris," Liam says while unsuccessfully trying to pick up a sushi roll with his chopsticks.

"Just ask for a fork and stop complaining," Alice replies. "At least here nobody is trying to kill you." They are eating in one of Tokyo's street restaurants.

"A fork?" Liam says. "I haven't seen a fork for over two weeks now. They have talking robots here in Japan but not forks!"

"If you don't stop complaining soon, I'll be the one to kill you!" Alice says. She opens her big blue eyes and looks at him seriously before she winks and smiles at him.

It's been over a month since Liam fell onto Alice's car. He feels bad that she got shot because of him, and he doesn't want to part from Alice until he's sure she's better—at least that's what he keeps telling himself and others. The truth is, he likes her more and more with each interaction. His superiors in the police department suggested that Liam take some time off and travel somewhere until things settle down a bit because this is the second time that someone has tried to kill him.

It doesn't take long for him to convince Alice to come with him. She's also trying to stay off the radar because The Nobodies might strike again, and having a police lieutenant next to her makes her feel much safer.

Alice finds Liam to be good looking, smart, and funny but she hasn't developed any deeper feelings for him. They are having fun together, hanging out, and having sex. Although Liam is quite excited about all of that, for Alice, it is merely a distraction. However, she does like spending time with him.

After they finish eating, Liam pays the bill, and they go back to their hotel.

"I love Tokyo!" Alice says as she throws her things on the table and then plunks herself on the sofa.

"Yeah, right," Liam says. "It's so busy and loud, and don't even get me started on the food!"

Alice scowls. "You're a mood killer, you know!"

"OK, OK, I'll stop complaining . . . If you kiss me!" He closes his eyes and puts his lips forward in expectation. He feels something cold and smooth slide down his lips and opens his eyes.

"There!" Alice says. "Now you're a pretty little lady who complains all the time!"

He realizes she just painted his lips with her red lipstick. Alice laughs while Liam tries to remove the lipstick and then runs to the bathroom to wash it off.

Liam feels a connection with Alice, and he's thinking of telling her about his theory and why people are trying to kill him. He knows it's too early, but he wants to speak with someone about it, and Alice seems like someone who can keep a secret and who would have no use for that information.

Little does he know . . .

"Listen, I want to share something with you," he says, "something personal."

"Do you think it's really necessary?" Alice replies. "I was thinking of taking a shower."

"Yeah, go for it. I can tell you as you do."

"OK, sure." She hopes he's not going to start expressing his emotions to her.

"I have a theory," he begins as she pulls some things out of the dresser drawer. "I've investigated a lot, and I've found a connection between some murders happening around the world. It looks like a lot of bad people have been murdered or have disappeared over the past few years. It seems like someone has been targeting these people and sending assassins to deal with it."

"I'm listening!" Alice says. She's in the bathroom now getting undressed but has left the door open to hear him better.

"The weird part is," Liam continues, "the assassins are just regular people with no previous criminal history, not even a parking ticket." Alice is now completely undressed and looking at herself in the mirror. She's starting to realize what Liam is talking about.

"I'm sure there's someone behind the curtain making all the decisions and paying a big chunk of money to these 'regular' people to execute the mission, but I can't figure out how they're communicating. However, ever since I went to my superiors with this information, I've been attacked twice."

Alice realizes that Liam is talking about The Nobodies. It's a perfect fit. The last time this topic came up with another man, she almost got killed. Her heart is pounding as she remembers that in the living room where Liam is, on the table in her purse, she still has Vitolicerin 12 hidden in a perfume bottle. She walks out of the bathroom, completely naked, and goes straight for her purse, pulling out the bottle.

"I forgot my perfume!" she says, waving the bottle.

Liam never gets tired of seeing her naked. Her breasts, her soft, shiny skin, her tiny, perfect waist. The only imperfection on her body is the bullet scar on her left thigh, which, in Liam's eyes, makes her even more perfect.

Liam stands up quickly and grabs the arm in which she's holding the bottle. "Please don't," he says. "I love your natural scent. Don't ruin it with perfume" He closes his eyes and slides his nose over her neck.

"Oh, trust me, this is the best perfume in the world. You're going to love it." She pulls her arm out of his hand and points the bottle of Vitolicerin 12 in his face.

Liam tilts his head back and flares his nostrils. "OK, let me smell it!"

Alice looks into his eyes as her index finger presses on the button at the top of the bottle. Then she stops. "You know what? I think I'll save it for a special occasion!" She returns it to her purse. *No, he isn't one of them,* she thinks. "I'm taking a shower now. Don't disturb me!" She wants to hide her teary eyes before Liam suspects something.

Liam sits on the couch, deep in thought as he waits for Alice to finish her shower.

He knows it's bad, but he's curious about how Alice's perfume smells. He reaches for her purse and pulls out the bottle.

He holds it close to his nose, but he can't smell anything. He knows that if he sprays it on his hand, Alice will smell it and find out what he did, so he takes a page from the small notepad on the table in the living room and sprays some of the perfume on it. He still can't smell anything. Liam holds the paper close to his nose and takes a deep breath. Still nothing.

He holds the bottle close, trying to read the brand and where it's from when he starts feeling dizzy. He tries to put the bottle back in her purse, but he loses strength and drops the bottle on the floor. It shatters as he loses consciousness and falls over a chair.

CHAPTER 25

The Poachers

Zimbabwe, Africa, October 2019

In a huge city hall building in Zimbabwe, thirty-five floors tall with one of the largest ballrooms in Africa, which can seat over two thousand people, a session is about to start. Some people in attendance know one other, and others don't, so a lot of small talks are taking place.

"I can't wait to see who organized this for us," a man named Garry says. "Finally, there's someone who appreciates what we do!"

"People don't understand the art of the animal business and their precious parts," his new friend, Mark, says. "I've been called a poacher for most of my life when, in fact, we're just businesspeople, am I right?" His conversation partners nod in agreement.

"Did you guys also receive an envelope with a generous amount inside just to join this session of appreciation, or did only I get one because I'm the best in the business?" Mario laughs, but he really wants to know the answer.

The others confirm that they also received an envelope with money inside.

"I didn't believe it at first," a guy named Mark says, "but then I got a call from Frank and Bob, and we figured, why not come? What's the worst that can happen? It's not like someone can arrest us here. There's no proof, plus the money is quite generous." The others all nod in agreement.

"Yeah, I like how everything is nicely organized," Garry says. "We even needed to leave our phones outside this room, which makes sense, so this can be completely anonymous in order to keep us all safe."

"Shhh," Mario says. "I think it's starting!"

Everyone falls silent as the lights dim, and a spotlight illuminates the stage. A handsome man in his late fifties appears. Before he can say a word, the applause from the over two thousand people in attendance fills the room as do a lot of "thank-yous" and whistles. He smiles mildly and then raises his hand to indicate he wants to talk. The room falls silent again.

"Gentlemen, I want to thank you for coming here from around the world. You are the best poachers in the world, and you have worked hard to earn that reputation." It's dark, but he sees people nodding all around the room. "In every business, sport, and job, you have the privilege to be called 'the best,' and I'm here today because I want to announce the best poacher in the world!"

The audience gets excited once again about being appreciated for what they do after such a long time!

"But first, say it out loud. What's your favorite beast for poaching?" His question is met by a chorus of replies.

"Leopards!"

"Rhinos!"

"Sharks!"

"Elephants, of course!"

"Alright then, let's play a game!" the man says. People are getting more excited. "On the right side of your arm-chairs are two buttons, a blue and a red one. I will start the countdown, and when I reach zero, press the blue button for 'elephant' and the red button for 'rhino!' All of you who guess which one of those two is my favorite beast to hunt will get a cash prize. The faster you answer—but not before I say zero—the higher the prize will be! Are you ready?"

"Yes!" the crowd replies, but no one applauds because they want to be ready to be the first one to answer correctly.

"All right," the man says. "Five . . . four . . . three . . . two . . . . one . . . zero!" His words are followed by a thousand clicking sounds.

The man is silent. He just stands there, watching. The audience is also silent.

What they don't realize is that each button, blue and red, is hiding a tiny needle. No matter what each person chose, they were got stung in the finger that they used to press the button.

"The correct answer to which beast I like to hunt most is . . . poachers," the man says. Suddenly, more people join him on stage, wearing masks of the most-poached animals in the world. "Have you ever, just for a millisecond thought about the pain the animals go through while you're carving them? Well, today is education day!"

The men in masks open their bags and pull out saws, knives, and machetes.

"You just sit tight and enjoy the show," the man says. "The poison mixture of the blue-ringed octopus and a dart frog will keep you paralyzed, but don't worry, you'll feel, everything." The room brightens as the lights are turned up.

The masked men spread out around the room and start pulling the poachers' teeth, cutting their ears off with machetes, and chopping off their fingers with small axes while making sure their victims look straight into the elephant, leopard, and rhino masks, ensuring they die in pain rather than killing them quickly by cutting some of their vital parts and making it easy.

Nearly two hours later, it's done. Two thousand poachers are now in ten thousand pieces.

The smell of blood is strong. It's one of the most horrific scenes that the man has ever seen, but his expression doesn't change over those two hours. He watches everything peacefully.

The masked men, about thirty in total, are exhausted. They have to kill the final few quickly because they are running out of strength and stamina.

The man looks up at the ceiling and nods. A moment later, the sound of silenced automatic gunfire comes from above, and the masked men fall over dead while bullets rip through them like they're made of paper.

It's over. Everyone in the room is dead except the man and the person with the machine gun, who is now climbing down.

They stand next to each other, surveying the room.

"It's a bit cruel, even for you," Gamba says. "Let's go; our chopper has arrived." He tosses the gun into the room amongst all the corpses.

"They're lucky they can only die once," Connor says. Then he turns and leaves the ballroom while pressing a button on a remote control that turns on a projector. On a huge screen behind the stage, it projects the following message:

"Heroes are good, but no one is afraid of them.
Villains, on the other hand . . ."

CHAPTER 26

Breaking News

Victor returns to his motel room, which is small and old and close to San Francisco airport. He checked in with a fake ID and paid in cash a few days ago. He thinks there's a slim chance that The Nobodies will search for him there. However, life plays games with everyone. He just had an encounter with Bogdan and his dog, both of them unaware of who the other person is.

He turns on the old TV, unable to believe it's actually in color. He doesn't really care what he watches. Most of the channels don't work. He just wants one with a decent picture. Victor notices his favorite WNC channel has a big red "BREAKING" sign at the bottom of the screen and turns up the volume. Everyone's favorite redhead, Natalie Archer, is on the screen.

"Over two thousand people reported dead in a conference center in Zimbabwe! There isn't a single survivor in the room painted in blood and horror! It's confirmed that all the people present at that secret conference were heavily involved in the poaching business. The police are confused because a message was left on a big screen in the room: "Heroes are good, but no one is afraid of them. Villains, on the other hand . . ." They are trying to discover who has the motive and the power to execute such an unprecedented massacre."

Could it be? Victor wonders. *The Nobodies?* After all, that's the goal, to eliminate bad people and maintain balance in the world. But over two thousand people on the same day and in the same spot?

He realizes it's been a month with no sign of Lucy and nobody trying to kill him yet, but if The Nobodies are capable of doing something like this, they can find him on the bottom of the ocean if they want to. Something has changed.

In his camper, Bogdan is watching YouTube on his mobile phone when he notices a lot of uploads and videos related to the Zimbabwe event.

He watches all of it and forms an opinion similar to Victor's, but he plans to be even more careful, thinking the Zimbabwe events might be just be a side mission.

He also thinks of Victor, the guy from the beach. They didn't introduce themselves formally, but he felt a different vibe coming from him. He isn't the kind of person who Bogdan meets every day in the dog park, and his dog had so many scars.

I better find out who that guy really is . . .

CHAPTER 27

Alice's World Of Lies

Alice folds her wet hair in a towel after showering and puts on a bathrobe before exiting the bathroom. While she showered, the hot, steamy water relaxing her body, she's thought about how open she should be with Liam. Could he actually help her? But no, she has only known him for a month. She had known David way longer, and he tried to kill her.

"You know, I was thinking . . ." she says as she walks out of the bathroom and then stops when she sees Liam on the floor. Alice looks around the room to see if anyone broke in and attacked him, but then she notices her perfume bottle broken on the floor not far from him.

"Oh, no, no, no! What have you done, you imbecile? Don't die on me here like this!" *I'm fucked,* she thinks, but she still wants to try and save Liam.

He opens his eyes slowly. Alice runs toward him and pulls him a few meters away from the broken bottle. "Hey, hey, talk to me," she says. "What did you do? Did you spray it? Inhale it? What? I can help you if you talk." She slaps his cheek with her hand.

"I . . . I smelled it," Liam says. "From that piece of paper . . ." He raises his hand and points at the paper. "You said it's exceptional, and I wanted to find out how it smelled." He's slowly recovering and becoming more aware. Alice is silent. She doesn't know what to say. It's obvious it isn't perfume, and she's hoping some "smart lie" will come to her fast.

"Wait . . ." Liam shakes her off and stands up shakily. "Who are you, and what's in that bottle?"

"My husband gave me that," Alice lies. "He said if I ever get attacked to spray it in the person's face, and it would work much better than pepper spray, knocking the attacker unconscious. He's a scientist." She realizes that more shit's coming because she never told him that she is/was married.

"You have a husband? What happened to him?" Liam asks, eyeing her suspiciously.

"Nothing. We had a little fight, and I left on a trip to France to cool off. We decided it's best for us to separate for a bit."

"But you've spent a month here in Tokyo with me. You're a bad liar!" She's a bit lost in her lies but figures it's less harmful to lie about her husband than admit she's part of The Nobodies.

"I'm still not sure what to do—return to him or stay with you!" She tries the "a good offense is the best defense" technique.

Liam stares at her as he shakes his head, trying to read her face. "Hmm . . . I don't know who to trust anymore, but I do like you, and you know that!" He steps toward her.

"I like you too," Alice replies, "but it's more complicated from my side." She softens her voice and tries to look vulnerable.

"All right, all right." Liam wraps her in a hug. They start kissing, and a few seconds later, Alice feels something cold around her wrists and hears a familiar clicking sound. She realizes she's handcuffed as Liam takes a few steps backward.

"Except I checked on you with my police computer. Your husband went missing the moment you left Australia, so I would say you've done something nasty, and you're on the run." He sits on the sofa, crosses his arms, and waits for Alice to start talking.

CHAPTER 28

The Very Bad People

"I'm not angry about what you did but because you didn't tell us," Vera says. She's visibly upset with Connor and Gamba as well because they didn't share their plans regarding the "Poachers Massacre," as it's now referred to.

"Is this how we're going to do things from now on?" Pierre asks. "Maybe Vera and I can't be trusted as much as Gamba." His feelings are obviously hurt as well.

"You guys are overreacting!" Gamba says, trying to calm them. "Connor asked me for a favor, and I owe him a couple. Plus, it was only a two-man job."

"It isn't about trust," Connor says calmly. "But I did think you guys might have tried to talk me out of it."

"Damn right!" Vera says. "What's that about?" She's getting angrier, and she's already on her second glass of vodka.

"It's what we spoke about during our last meeting," Connor says, looking at Pierre.

"So you've already started your 'big project,' Pierre r says. You don't need us anymore?" He's still a bit insulted at being left out.

Connor sighs. "Guys, we need to increase our numbers. We can't keep eliminating only two or three bad people per month. We're falling behind."

"So now we're going to kill hundreds of millions of them?" Vera asks mockingly.

"More than that, if needed!" Connor says.

"See, Connor, I wanted to help you with the thing in Zimbabwe. It's 'my Africa,' and poachers are destroying its most magnificent beauty: animals and nature. But more than that, I'm a bit unsure." Gamba is seeking to justify his recent actions.

"That's a bit selfish, don't you think?" Connor says. "You're prioritizing your people over everyone else." Gamba wants to respond, but Connor continues. "Listen, if I'm the only one who is seeing the greater good in all this, so be it. No one is forcing you to do anything. The scumbags who died in Zimbabwe deserved it, and you know it. The upcoming years will show an improvement in the number of endangered animals, which means nature will be healthier, and the food chain will balance out. Certain things need to stop now, and if I'm being honest to you, this isn't even one percent of what I'm planning to do."

They all stare at him. For the first time they think that maybe they're not following him.

"By the look in your eyes, I see you disagree with all of this, but that's alright. That's why I'm leaving this committee, so you guys don't have to be connected to future actions like this."

They are a bit shocked, but they're also slightly relieved. They all thought it was a bit too much, preventing them from going to bed at night with a peaceful mind. The others don't know what to say. Everything is a bit confusing. Their meetings don't usually end this way.

"But I will ask you two things, as a lifelong friend," Connor says. They all lean in closer, anxious to hear. "Never interfere with any of my future missions, and I will keep control of all Nobodies."

"How do we know these hundreds of millions of people you're planning to kill, don't include some of our family and friends?" Vera asks.

"Are any of your friends very bad people?" Connor asks.

There is a moment of silence before Vera answers, looking around the table at all three guys. "Yes," she says. "All of them."

CHAPTER 29

The Black Bunny

Guangzhou, China, October 2019, a few hours after Connor leaves the committee

It's the most populous city in China with over forty-four million people, and it looks like they're all out on the streets. A huge music festival is underway. It's nearly midnight, but it's almost as bright as day because the lights and special effects from DJ Zheng are on another level, making Guangzhou look like the biggest nightclub in the world.

People are dressed in all kinds of funny attire, including masks, sparkly clothes, and electric sunglasses in all colors.

A man with a black bunny gas mask is dancing by himself, and by the look of him, he's having way too much fun. He's jumping around to the rhythm of the song when he reaches the area where the fog is coming on during the most exciting parts of the songs. The man pulls something out of his pocket and places it inside the black fog machine and then continues hopping around. He goes to another fog machine and does the same thing.

Soon all forty fog machines have a mysterious substance inside. Then the man hops back into the middle of the crowd and continues to party.

"Are you readyyyyy?" DJ Zheng yells into the microphone.

"Yes!" the crowd replies as the lights go down.

The music stops for a moment, and then, like an explosion, lights of all colors turn on, the music starts rocking, and the fog machines fill the air. As the beat pounds, fifty thousand people inhale the infected fog.

The man with the black bunny gas mask dances like never before.

CHAPTER 30

A Life For A Life

In one chair is Liam—calm, curious, and ready for Alice to start talking. In another is Alice, her hands cuffed behind her back, lost in her lies, and looking for a way out of her situation.

She thinks of screaming, so the hotel staff might hear her, but then he can pull out his police badge and tell them whatever he wants. A few more things come to mind, but then Alice thinks about telling the truth and hoping for Liam's understanding because she's already too stressed by the situation.

"You're right about your investigation," Alice says slowly.

"About what exactly?" Liam asks. He didn't expect that this situation would be connected with that.

"Just a few years back, in my hometown of Alice Springs in Australia, a big forest fire threatened our city. I lived there with my father because my mother divorced him a couple of years before that, and she said that if I chose to stay with my father in Australia, I had chosen him over her, and she would never contact me again. It was an easy choice because I'd never felt a strong connection with my mom like I had it with my dad. It's weird, but she was always at work.

"Like everyone else, my father and I tried to help save as many animals as possible from burning alive. My father noticed a mother and a baby koala on a burning tree and rushed toward it when another flaming tree fell on him and nailed him to the ground."

"My father started to burn alive, unable to move due to the weight of the tree. I stood there watching in horror, frozen in place, unable the move.

"Luckily, a few local people rushed in with fire extinguishers, and while three people lifted the tree, one person managed to pull my dad out.

"A few hours later, a doctor at the hospital informed me that my father suffered third-degree burns and would need a long and expensive surgery, and when I saw the cost, I realized I couldn't pay it even in my dreams. He was dying, but I was completely useless. I thought that if there was anything I could do to save my father, I would do it. Anything."

Liam watches her, listening carefully as Alice continues. "A man who I had never seen before sat next to me and without asking any question or introducing himself let me know that he could easily pay for the surgery out of his pocket and if I was interested that I should meet him in the smoking area outside the hospital.

"Of course, I didn't care who he was or how he suddenly knew about my father's surgery and everything, and I went straight out there. He got straight to the point, explaining that his organization would take care of all costs, including surgery and recovery, if I would do a few things for them, some of which might involve taking other people's lives. But he said all the people would deserve it and that I shouldn't feel bad about it. 'A life for a life,' he said. He gave me ten seconds to think about it, and I told him I would do whatever it took to save my father."

Liam becomes increasingly focused as Alice relays her story. "Everything was done in a few days. The surgery was successful, my father was recovering, and I spoke with the doctors to make sure my father wasn't on the hook for expenses because 'his cousin' had paid and didn't want to make my father feel like he needed to return the favor."

"They didn't contact me for a few weeks. I figured they were giving me some time to spend with my dad. But then I received a call explaining how to download a mobile app called The Nobodies and how they would communicate with me through it."

Liam raises his eyebrows in surprise. "A mobile app?"

Alice nods. "A game. It's an app that they use to communicate with us. My first mission was to seduce and marry a person named David Hill, my ex-husband."

"And then they asked you to kill him?" Liam liked to play the detective and tried to guess the end of the story.

Alice sighed. "I wish it were as simple as that. Me marrying David was all about me having easy access to the highly effective poison that he produced, and then it all started.

"Since then I've been asked to, well, kill a few people, which I did. However, as promised, they were all horrible people: drug dealers, rapists, murderers . . . They also paid me a lot of money for each mission in addition to paying for my dad's surgery. It's easy for me to do what they ask, and I've never thought of going to the police. I don't know if I can say that I enjoy it, but I don't hate it."

"It doesn't make any sense," Liam says, thinking out loud. "Powerful people like that can hire a professional assassin, so why you? But then again, nobody would see you coming. You don't look like a professional killer, and you're a beautiful woman, with some deadly poison to help you out. Sure, I see . . . What happened to your father?"

"He met a Spanish woman, Maria, fell in love, and after I married David, he went with her to live in Madrid. He said to me, 'Ali, the woman loves me with all these scars. I better take this opportunity.' He's happy with her."

"And your husband?"

"He tried to kill me, but I killed him first. It turned out he was also a member of The Nobodies."

"Why did they try to get rid of you if you were doing such a great job for them?"

"I killed an innocent man," Alice says. "One of the security guards from David's company. He saw me taking the poison from the lab. I didn't know it then, but I'm sure it's because of that. There isn't anything else."

As Liam looks at her, so many feelings are flowing through his body. He almost wants to pinch himself to make sure he isn't dreaming. He's proud that he's right about his investigation, but he sees Alice differently now. She's a hitman .

"I would be the worst cop in the world not to arrest you after admitting to all these murders," he says.

"I don't see how that will solve anything," Alice says, "but it's your call."

They look at each other in silence. Then someone knocks on the door. "Room service!"

Liam looks at Alice. "Did you order something?"

She shakes her head slowly. "No . . ."

CHAPTER 31

The Team

Victor goes to the same dog beach for a few days, sitting on a rock just watching the waves and thinking. Leo lies next to him, chewing a large tree branch that he found nearby.

Victor is thinking about how it has been a while, and he still has no clues that will lead him to Lucy. He's wondering about his next move and what he needs to do in order to make progress in that field.

Victor keeps repeating the story in his head. Lucy went into the woods, and after that he and Leo were attacked by wolves. She's gone, and he feels so powerless. She could be anywhere.

In the Nobodies app, there's no way of contacting them back, so he keeps returning to the dog beach, hoping they will find him, so he can at least try to communicate.

It's been approximately a month, and he's already frustrated with this type of life, hiding and then hoping they'll find him. Also, without Lucy, he starts questioning if this is all worth it, to hide for the rest of his life. He wonders if he can just get the most difficult and dangerous task in the world from The Nobodies, and if he accomplishes it, he can get out, and they will let him live in peace. He doesn't even want any money. He just wants to get Lucy back and for them to stop contacting him.

Yes, that would be perfect.

Victor looks over his right shoulder and notices the same guy with the same dog from the other day. He thinks he can use some company for him and Leo for a few minutes, just to stop thinking for a moment.

Leo stands up as D approaches. They sniff each other, and then D starts provoking Leo to play. Leo looks at Victor for approval and Victor motions for Leo to go and play with her.

"No judo moves today, hey?" Bogdan says. He looks at Victor but doesn't raise his hand for a handshake. "I'm Sergei. Nice to meet you." He wants to remain careful until he knows more.

"James," Victor replies. "Nice to meet you." Victor is thinking along the same lines as Bogdan.

They turn around to see what Leo and D are doing. They're chasing each other and wrestling.

"One of the warmest days in San Francisco for sure," Bogdan says, removing his leather jacket.

"Must be. Even here next to the water it's warm, which is unusual." He scans Bogdan's arms, which are full of tattoos. "I've thought of getting one as well."

Bogdan glances at his arms. "A tattoo?"

"Yes, but just one, and it would probably be a portrait of my dog. I know, not very creative." He smiles, expecting a funny comment about it from "Sergei."

"Well, I do think tattoos should have meaning. Otherwise, you're just doing it to show off, so a dog tattoo sounds pretty good to me." He smiles as well. "Now you gave me an idea. I might tattoo at least a letter D as her nickname or something."

"If you still have some space left," Victor says, and they both chuckle.

Their mobile phones both make a sound announcing they have received a notification. They look at each other, put their hands in their pockets, and pull out their mobile phones.

They have each received a message from The Nobodies, which makes them instantly become serious and sharper.

Victor's message is as follows.

> Dear Victor,
>
> We have decided to remove you from our missions and the Nobodies list, which means you'll no longer be hunted by us, and you'll no longer be employed by us. And yes, Lucy is safe and sound, and she will be given back to you as well."
>
> However, we need you to complete one final mission, the details of which will be sent to you if you accept the offer.
>
> Think, we can eliminate you at any time. We know every step you take and every place you visit with your dog, but we won't. This is your way out.
>
> To start with, you'll need to work together with the man who is currently standing next to you, Bogdan Morozov. Stay close to each other, and we will send you the

final mission details if you click "accept" in
the next five minutes.

He lifts his head and notices "Sergei," a.k.a. Bogdan, is
looking at him with a question in his eyes.

Bogdan has received a similar message. They both stand
up and look around, but no one else is on the beach. They
are curious if someone is observing them from afar.

"So, Bogdan, did we get similar messages?" Victor asks.
He can feel the tension.

"I came back to this beach looking for you," Bogdan
says. "I was right. My gut told me that I should do that. And
yes, if they asked you to work with me, then my message
is similar."

"They will leave you in peace afterward. Did they say
that too?"

Bogdan nods. "Yes."

"Do you trust them?"

"No."

"Do you have a choice?"

"No . . ."

"Me neither." Victor raises his mobile phone and
presses "accept."

"Looks like they always get what they want," Bogdan
says and then does the same.

CHAPTER 32

The Smallest Killer

Underground laboratory,
unknown location, November 2019,

An automatic glass door opens, and Connor goes through it, approaching one of the world's top scientists, if not the best, Tao Woo, who has been working for Connor for nearly three decades.

"Mr. Jones, welcome," Tao says. "It's a great pleasure to meet you! Today is the big day, or should I say, the biggest?" The small, white-haired Chinese man in his late seventies is filled with excitement.

"Thank you, Mr. Woo," Connor says. "Is it ready?" He's a bit nervous.

"Everything is ready for you to see it with your own eyes and approve it! Please follow me."

Tao has been working for Connor for twenty-four years in this laboratory, but this is the first time they've met personally. Connor chose to finally show himself for this experiment. He needs to see it with his own eyes. Tao has invested twenty-four years into this single big project and a few minor ones, and he has announced to Connor that it's now safe to launch it.

Not many people in the world can be cold like Connor, but at this moment, his hands are shaking, and he starts sweating due to excitement as Tao Woo leads him down the hallway.

"I watched WNC the other day," Tao says. "Looks like that poison mix that I sent you worked just fine." He's referring to the poison used in the Poachers Massacre.

"I never doubted it would. Thank you, Mr. Woo." Connor was raised to address older people with respect. Tao Woo likes that about Connor. Yes, he likes the money as well, but the main reason he works for him is that Tao Woo truly believed in Connor and his projects the moment they spoke over the phone twenty-four years ago.

Connor had the entire lab built just for Tao Woo and then executed every single builder after the laboratory was done so that only the two of them knew about it.

"And the 'virus' that we implemented in Guangzhou," Tao says, "it's just a matter of time, and we're going to be hearing about it on TV. Are you sure we don't need to do the same in India?"

Connor shakes his head. "That isn't necessary. The few thousand Indians attending that event will carry the virus back to their country when they return from the festival."

Tao nods. "Very well."

"You mentioned this only works on Indian and Chinese genes, correct? Other nationalities cannot get infected by it?"

"Correct, Mr. Jones."

"Not even if just one parent is from one of those countries?"

"Not even then, Mr. Jones."

Connor looks at the small old man walking in front of him and thinks, *What a genius.*

"Here we are," Tao says. "Please, Mr. Jones, remove your jacket, and proceed inside the testing room." He points him into a room that's made entirely of transparent material, probably a mixture of glass and plastic. It's the size of a basketball court.

Ten people are tied to chairs, tape on their mouths, blindfolds on their eyes, and earphones with the loud music in their ears, so they can't hear what's happening around them. Connor removes his jacket, revealing his black Metallica T-shirt. He's very muscular for his age.

The door closes, and after Connor sits on the eleventh chair next to all the people who are tied up, he nods to Tao Woo to start the experiment.

A small window opens, and thousands of mosquitos fly into the room. The mosquitos cover the people who are tied to the chairs. It lasts no longer than one minute, and then the mosquitoes fly back through the same window from which they came.

Connor gets up to examine the people tied to the chairs. He approaches the first one from the left. He has lots of mosquito bites, and he's shaking in shock. Connor looks at the little card tied to his chair. It says "Drugs."

Connor moves on to the next person. His card says "HIV virus."

The third card says "Cigarettes."

The fourth man doesn't have a single mosquito bite. Connor looks at his card. It says "Clean." He looks at Tao through the glass, wondering if he has finally done it.

The other cards of the men who have large numbers of bites say "Tuberculosis" and other extremely deadly and contagious diseases. The word "Alcohol" is on the card of a person with many bites. The same goes for the people with cards that read "Zika," "Malaria," and other types of deadly, highly transmittable diseases.

Like Connor, the people with "Clean," "Regular flu," and "Cancer" on their cards don't have a single bite.

Connor can't believe it. After twenty-four years, it looks like it's finally complete!

He walks out of the exam room. "You're a world hero, Mr. Tao Woo."

"I merely executed your idea, which is brilliant!" Tao is a humble man, though he appreciates the praise.

"How long until the bitten victims die?" Connor asks.

"The timing depends on the number of bites," Tao says, "but death is certain. No longer than a week."

Connor nods "Good. Tell me more about them."

"As requested, they feed on the regular female mosquitos, so if you approve the mass breading production, their numbers should increase dramatically, considering that because of female mosquitos, this planet loses seven hundred and fifty thousand people a year due to malaria, dengue, zika, and similar diseases. These mosquitos we have created will save half a million lives per year at a minimum! "

"But they will take another one hundred million lives," Connor says.

"Well, these mosquitos carefully select their victims according to the level of drugs, nicotine, or alcohol in the blood and the deadly and transmittable diseases that individuals are carrying. No innocent people will die."

Connor doesn't respond. He knows he can't say that someone is "not innocent" if by accident he or she gets one of the deadly diseases. He knows that many innocent people will die, but he believes it is absolutely necessary for this planet, and the number of people who deserve it will be way higher.

"They are extremely fast," Tao says, "as you have witnessed. And they are ten times harder to kill than regular mosquitos. Their body structure allows them to be slapped by a human hand and still have a fifty percent chance of full recovery. They attack their victims, and when the job is done, they move on to the next. They sleep one hour a day, and they never stay still apart from that hour of sleep."

"You're an incredible scientist, Mr. Tao Woo. Please send me the entire description of them down to the tiniest details, and I'll let you know the next step." He turns to leave.

"Wait, Mr. Jones, one thing is missing!" Tao says. Connor eyes him curiously. "An incredible mosquito like this needs a name. They are going to change the future of the world, so they deserve it!"

"Mr. Woo, you have spent the last twenty-four years creating them, so there is no one else who deserves to name them more than you."

"Very well then. They fly, they take lives, they save lives, and they're white. The Angel Mosquitos!"

Connor just smiles.

CHAPTER 33

Against An Old Friend

An unknown location in Switzerland,
early December, 8 p.m.

Vera is in her home, sitting comfortably in her armchair. She reaches for the remote to turn on her TV.

She plays the Worldwide News Channel (WNC), which always has the most updated information about the latest events around the world. Vera knows that if Connor has made any moves, this is one of the best ways to find out about it because this is what he wants, the world to know the consequences and to act and behave better. Stunning anchor Natalie Archer is going over some major events.

"The massacre in Zimbabwe is still a mystery. Two months later, Zimbabwean police, together with a multinational police task force, are still looking for these ruthless criminals, although many animal lovers around the world support the act. It's a top priority for police to find the people who did it.

"We are also receiving news from China that in Guangzhou, doctors have discovered a new virus. So far, doctors are still investigating; however, the hospitals are full, and there are eleven confirm deaths already. More on this topic in our morning program tomorrow."

She moves on to some other topics, but Vera finds them irrelevant. *That new virus in China,* she thinks. *It might be him. 1.5 billion people, overpopulation . . .* She looks at her phone and considers calling Connor. After all, they have been friends for almost her entire life. Just as she's trying to decide what to do, the phone rings, which scares her for a moment, but she picks up the receiver. It's a secure line that only The Nobodies use.

"Yes?" she asks carefully.

"Hi," Pierre says. "I have G on the line as well." He means that Gamba is on the call. Even with the secure line, they don't want to use any names.

"Yes I'm here," Gamba says. "What's up?" His voice is flat.

"Are you guys watching WNC?" Pierre asks. "Are we on the same page on this new virus in China situation?" He knows they are both watching.

"We're thinking about the same person; that's for sure," Vera says.

"It might be a coincidence," Gamba says, testing them.

"I don't think so," Pierre replies confidently.

"Well, even if it is," Vera says, "why does that concern us?"

"We're still The Nobodies, aren't we?" Pierre asks, raising his voice.

"What do you suggest?" Gamba asks calmly.

"I think we should meet," Pierre says.

"To discuss what?" Vera asks.

"Are we still here to maintain the balance now that there's no more committee?" Pierre asks. "We need to protect the world from the biggest villains, as always. Nothing has changed, even if the biggest villain is one of our friends."

"Send the car," Vera says, then hangs up.

"Do it," Gamba agrees.

When one of them decides on a location, a driver is sent to bring them to the meeting's location. They have always trusted each other, and it has worked for a few decades now. They will never benefit in case of one other's death. They are all important to each other due to their incredible connections.

Vera feels uncomfortable about the meeting though, as if they're cheating on Connor. She doesn't have a good feeling about it.

CHAPTER 34

The Virus

It is, in fact, room service, as they introduced themselves through the door to Alice and Liam. However, they are delivering not food but an envelope with Alice's name on it. She takes the letter and opens it.

Dear Alice,

We hope that you have enjoyed your little vacation in France and Japan. We wanted to give you some rest and time to think about everything. We didn't alert the Australian police in regard to the murder of your husband, and we're not planning to.

However, we're preparing for the last big project, and we have an important role for you to play. In fact, we have an important role for Lieutenant Mercier as well. This task will close our partnership, and we're ready to let you both go on with your normal lives if the task is completed successfully.

You don't need to answer immediately. Please download the app again on your phone, so we don't need to contact you with letters anymore in the future. The mission will be sent to you in the next few weeks, so you have plenty of time to think it over.

Meanwhile, both of you are safe from our side if the lieutenant will stop digging up information on us.

Stay safe, and we will speak to you soon.

Alice and Liam read the letter together. They decide to wait and see what the task is and then make a decision from there.

They realize from the letter that so far The Nobodies know every step they have made. Liam decides to put his investigation on hold, realizing this might be too big. Even with Alice as proof that such an organization exists, there are too many clues to follow and people to be considered as suspects. *This is all so well organized*, he thinks. He doesn't give up completely, but he steps back for a moment.

They return to France, realizing there's no point in trying to hide anymore. They are in a relaxing bar in Paris when Liam sees something on TV and asks the bartender to turn up the volume for a second.

Natalie Archer is talking. "It seems the virus is spreading fast, and doctors believe it can be transferred through the air as much as through human contact. Doctors believe this virus was born in Guangzhou around two months ago and has been slowly taking lives ever since. It's called the Meng Virus, which means 'Dream Virus.' It's called that because there are no major symptoms, and victims mostly die in their sleep.

"Some victims experience tiredness, lie down to take a rest, and don't wake up anymore. It's painless, but it's also very, very scary. Doctors are saying that in the previous two months, over twenty thousand people have died from it, but it's difficult to say correct numbers because many families thought their loved ones died from natural causes. The biggest discovery of all is that all the victims are Chinese or Indian.

"Experts say it's almost impossible for a virus to aim at a certain race, but the fact is, all the unfortunate people who have died from it are either Chinese or Indian. Both countries are starting to consider the situation as very dangerous, but so far they are hesitating in their response because there is so much conflicting information on the table as doctors try to get to the bottom of this. The fact is, people are dying in their sleep, and no one knows where it came from or when it's going to stop."

"It looks like the new decade is going to be a fun one!" the bartender says, turning the volume down.

Liam and Alice look at each other. They feel something bad is going to happen, and The Nobodies have their fingers in it.

CHAPTER 35

The Beginnings

Bogdan and Victor are up to date with all the news about the Meng Virus, the Poachers Massacre, and everything else happening around the world.

They also know who is responsible for it all.

They have spent a month in San Francisco waiting for The Nobodies to contact them again with the final task. Victor and Bogdan are both hesitant to open up to each other at the beginning even though they realize they might need to work together to complete the final task, but as time passes, like their dogs, they become better friends by the day.

Bogdan gets a room in the same motel as Victor. They hang out often and talk about casual things. Tonight, they are in Victor's place. While the dogs lie next to each other sleeping, for the first time, the two men delve into a more personal conversation.

"How many people have you killed for them?" Victor asks.

Bogdan hesitates for a moment. "Twelve. You?"

"Eleven for them. The twelfth was their messenger. They asked me to kill my dog to prove my loyalty, so I killed one of their 'dogs' instead."

Bogdan looks at D. "I could never do it. She's all I have in this world."

Victor nods "Same here." He stops. "And Lucy, if she's still alive."

"How did you feel when you killed your first target?" Bogdan asks. It isn't an easy question, but he wants to compare Victor's reaction to how he felt the first time.

"I felt like it didn't really happen," Victor says. "It worried me because I felt nothing." His eyes become smaller and voice fainter.

"That's interesting," Bogdan says. "I actually puked on the body of my first victim." He's a bit embarrassed.

Victor nods. "I thought I would. I was sure while I was driving to his place that I would puke afterward. I even brought some plastic bags along just in case." They both chuckle.

"We can't be normal, can we?" Bogdan looks Victor in the eyes.

Victor frowns. "How do you mean?"

"In the night, you take someone's life, you kill a person, and in the morning, you go to work, like nothing happened. You run your restaurant, and me, I play football." His eyes are focused on his hands.

"I know why that is," Victor says confidently.

"Why?" Bogdan asks, looking up in surprise.

"Well, in my case, I already had that conversation with myself. It's a long one, and I would read the things that The Nobodies sent about the target over and over. Rapist, murderer, drug dealer, human trafficker . . . I would convince myself that I was doing the world a favor."

Bogdan nods in agreement. "Yeah, that's what makes me feel better too."

Victor's face falls. "Or maybe we're just lying ourselves. Who knows?"

"I don't think so," Bogdan replies. "Look, you can't kill your dog, right? You didn't even consider it. I bet you couldn't kill a regular person just for the money either."

Victor nods slowly. "I guess. All I want, like you, is my freedom—and, of course, for Lucy to come home."

"It must be hard, but don't lose hope. Chances are slim, but if we actually pull off whatever they ask of us, they might keep their word and let us live the rest of our lives in peace."

"Do you really believe that?" Victor asks. "Do you think they will ever leave us alone, no matter what we do?"

Bogdan gets a faraway look in his eye. "I've always thought of doing that last task, and then I would be free. Now that they've actually offered it, I have to try."

Victor can tell he's not convinced, but he has no other options. Victor can't blame him. He feels similar. It isn't fear; it's the uncomfortable feeling of looking over his shoulder and never letting himself relax and enjoy things, always being on his toes, scared to be happy and let his guard down because if he does, it could be his last time.

"How did you even got into this Nobodies thing?" Victor asks, standing up and walking toward the faucet.

"Well, I grew up in an orphanage, so everything was a bit harder for me: finding a job, making friends. I never knew my parents. Of course, to me they were very bad people, but the director of the orphanage once told me that they left a good amount of money for me when I turned eighteen and left the orphanage, so I could start my life. He was right.

They left me fifty thousand dollars to start with. Not bad at all."

"Wow," Victor says as he fills a glass with water. "If your parents had that much money to spare, why did they leave you in the first place?"

"I thought the same. It made me even angrier. In fact, I was so angry that I didn't take the money."

Victor looks at him in surprise. "So what did you do?"

"The director of the orphanage helped me start training in a football club. I liked it, but the money was barely enough for food and rent. All the other guys had more money, so they could afford to just play and not have a job on the side. I managed on only my football salary for a few years." He smiles sarcastically.

"You needed to find a job on the side to support you?" Victor asks, then sets down his empty glass and rejoins Bogdan.

Bogdan shakes his head. "No, because The Nobodies showed up. They invited me to do some 'jobs' for them and said I would have more money than any of my teammates and many other people in Russia. With the money they were offering, I would be more in line with the football club owners than my teammates.

"I didn't really believe it until everything actually started and I had killed a man—a punk, a drug dealer, the one that I puked on afterward. I think they were testing me, to see if I could really do it."

Victor nods. "Makes sense. My first target was also a street-level drug dealer. What happened after that?"

"I found a bag full of money when I returned home, and that was my 'Holy shit, this is the real deal' moment. On the side, I continued to play football. It was a perfect cover, and on top of that, I loved it." He crosses his arms.

"I would agree," Victor says. "In the beginning, it was, 'Wow, holy shit!' But after, when I got a bit more mature, I was thinking, what do I need to do to get out of it? And I developed more of a conscience about my actions."

Bogdan nods in agreement. "How about you? How did you get in?"

"When my Grandpa Luigi died, they used that moment somehow. I was full of anger, like you, mad at the world, at God. I wanted to provide more for my family, and I did just that. I whacked a drug dealer for them, and, like you, I became aware that this shit was real when I found the money in the bag."

"What did you do with the body?" Bogdan asks, genuinely curious.

Victor chuckles. "You might find this weird or scary, but my Grandpa Luigi had a disposal hole in the garage that he made personally."

Bogdan's eyes widen. "A disposal hole?"

"Yes, like in the Italian mafia movies. You know, when the mafia kills someone and throws the body into a meat grinder, and his body is never found, so there's no murder, right? I think maybe Grandpa Luigi used it to dispose of old tires and stuff."

"Your grandpa was scary!" Bogdan says. They both chuckle. "Why in the world would your grandpa have something like that in his garage?"

Victor shrugs. "Hey, I don't know. He was Italian!" They have a good laugh at that. Then Bogdan narrows his eyes at Victor.

"Think he ever used it? The way you did, I mean."

Victor shrugs. "Not that I know of, but then, why would he build it in the first place? It must have taken a lot of time!"

They both fall silent, thinking for a moment.

"How did they kidnap your wife?" Bogdan asks. He looks at the dogs. "Does that have something to do with Leo's scars?"

They stay up till 4:00 a.m. sharing some of their most personal stories as they feel they might have actually found a friend in each other.

Who else could understand the life of a Nobody better than another Nobody?

CHAPTER 36

Goodbye, Old Friend(s)

Vera's car arrives in front of the small house in the woods.

The procedure is usually four cars and four drivers, but in this case without Connor, three drivers bring Gamba, Vera, and Pierre to the secure location for their meeting. The drivers work for all of them, so they can be trusted by each member of the committee.

The driver opens the door and helps Vera out of the car. Vera stands for a moment and looks at the house. She has done this a million times, but she still has a bad feeling about this one. They all know Connor, but she knows him the best. He would not mind them meeting without him, but if his name and actions are the main topic, it might not end well.

There's nothing else around, just a forest and the road that they used to reach the house. *Well, it's a secure location*, she thinks.

She never knows if she's the first or the last to arrive, so she heads into the house after the driver searches her and allows her to take, as usual, a small flask of vodka inside. Usually, a small glass is waiting for her on the table.

Pierre and Gamba are already inside. Vera notices a small rock glass on the table and realizes that's her seat. She's already opening her flask and pouring the vodka as she sits.

"You know, that might be too strong for your age now," Pierre says. "Drinking might kill you one day." He smiles as Vera finishes what's in the glass in one sip, then sets her glass on the table.

"Get serious," she says. "And let's get through this quickly."

"Why quickly?" Gamba asked. "You look stressed." He's in good spirits.

"I'm not." She looks at Pierre. "You called the meeting, so talk."

"Yes, of course," Pierre says. "So, my friends, we have a little situation here. My sources have confirmed that Connor is the one guilty of creating the so-called Meng Virus."

Vera waves her hand. "We already know that."

"Yes, but we needed to make sure in order to take the next step," Gamba says, placing his elbows on the table.

Vera pauses as she prepares to pour another shot. "What would that be?"

Pierre takes a breath before speaking. "See, I don't feel safe with all these viruses and mass killings knowing that Connor is around doing whatever he wants. Do you, Gamba?"

Gamba shakes his head. "Not at all." Vera observes the two men. Gamba is always in good spirits, but Pierre usually isn't. She starts suspecting something.

"Are you too scared to say it?" she asks.

The other two look at each other and laugh. That's the moment Vera knows something is wrong.

Pierre smiles proudly. "Let's just say Emilio might be knocking on Connor's door at this very moment." Vera's face turns serious.

"You didn't!" she says angrily.

Gamba leans forward. "Listen, Vera, sometimes you need to move on. Connor is losing it. I mean, him against the world? What is that? Suddenly, he's a mass murderer? No, that isn't normal."

Vera looks at them in disbelief. "After so many years, you just made a decision to kill a friend, and you didn't even ask my opinion? Who chose you as a leader?" She looks at Pierre, furious, her hands folded into fists.

"We thought you might react this way," Pierre says, remaining relaxed. "You've always admired Connor more than any of us. We know that a few times you've even seen each other without the two of us."

Vera puts her hands to her face. "You fools!"

"This isn't the way we wanted you to go, but it's inevitable," Gamba says. Vera looks at him in confusion.

"Where am I going?" She looks at Pierre and Gamba and then at the glass from which she's been drinking. "What did you do!"

"After Connor dies, we know you will not let that go, and we will need to look over our shoulders for the rest of our lives. So, we decided you must go with him to the 'better place.'"

"You know how Vitolicerin 12 works," Gamba explains patiently. "Soon you'll pass out, die, and we'll bury you in these woods. We will do that much for the sake of the long friendship we've had."

Vera doesn't have any weapons. She thinks of a few scenarios of breaking the vodka flask, but then she starts feeling dizzy, and her sight becomes blurry. She holds onto the table to prevent herself from falling out of her chair, but soon her strength runs out.

Everything is in slow motion and a bit blurry, but the last thing she sees before she passes out are the bullets splitting the smiling faces of Pierre and Gamba as they fall next to her with the majority of their heads and faces missing and pieces of brain scattered all over the floor.

CHAPTER 37

I Need A Favor

Vera opens her eyes, her vision is foggy, but it slowly becomes clear, and she notices Connor sitting on her right side as a guy in front of them digs a hole in the soil.

"What the hell happened?" Vera asks, still a bit dizzy.

"How are you feeling?" Connor asks quietly.

"My head is exploding. What happened?" She looks a bit disoriented.

"Pierre and Gamba sent Emilio to kill me. You know that, right?"

Vera nods. "I found out earlier. I didn't know they were planning that." She hangs her head, thinking she's also in trouble.

"I know. I was listening to the conversation. I was hoping you had nothing to do with it. Makes me happy that that's the case." He smiles.

Vera looks up. "But what happened to Emilio? How did you escape?"

Connor nods at the man. "He's right there, digging a hole. You don't recognize him?" Emilio stops shoveling for a moment and waves at Vera.

"Wait . . ." She zooms in with her small blue eyes, her vision having returned to normal. "OK, I'm lost right now. What's Emilio doing here?"

"Pierre and Gamba's plan of eliminating me might have worked, but they hired Emilio for that mission, which was their only mistake. I've never told any of you this, but Emilio is one of my good friends. He let me know, and he asked if he could take care of them."

"I see," Vera says, piecing it together in her mind. "How am I alive? You gave me the antidote?"

Connor nods. "Yes. To clarify, you don't owe me anything. I was happy to help."

On the contrary, Vera knows she owes him everything. "How did you listen to the conversation?" she asks.

"Your driver. He placed a small microphone in your right pocket while helping you out of the car."

"So you knew the location beforehand. This was all planned in advance. I don't even want to know more details, to be honest. Tell me, what are you going to do with me?"

"Well, I need a favor . . ."

Vera nods, "Go on." She knew something like this was coming.

"I was thinking, New Year's Eve is next week. Do you want to spend it with me?" He smiles softly at her.

CHAPTER 38

Tasks For Nobodies

There are only ten Nobodies left. Connor keeps the last ten that he considers to be the best fit for his big project. He has final tasks ready for all of them and has promised that this will be their last mission.

Luca Rosso, an Italian assassin, is a handsome guy with a serious face and long, shiny hair. He's reading his last mission in the Nobodies app. To sum up the message, he's to kill the North Korean Supreme Leader, Min-Jun. Connor found out that Min-Jun is in the final stages of planning a nuclear attack on the USA, which will take place in July 2020 at the latest.

Nathan Hart is an Englishman who wanted to be in the army but failed the personality exam three times. The English army doesn't know what a deadly soldier they failed to recruit. The tall, blond man with wide shoulders and a short beard is a weapons expert. His mission is to kill Russian Prime Minister Kiril Smirnov, who is plotting the murder of the Russian President and working with North Korea on the US attack in July 2020.

Klaus Bierhof is a German pilot/assassin. With his small blue eyes and lean body, he is quite popular with ladies. Connor recruited Klaus because he can fly anything— plane, chopper, even a hot-air balloon. He's the best at it. His mission is to bombard the villa of the Mexican drug lord, Esteban Rojo, including his drug fields and hangars full of drugs in Colombia, on the night when all the heads of all the biggest Latin cartels are celebrating together.

Branimir Lazic, a Serbian assassin, is fearless and professional and is the best sniper in the world. He has a cold face, dark eyebrows, a strong chin, and is always freshly shaved. He became the general of an illegal army when he was just thirty years old. He's the only Nobody who makes Emilio uncomfortable with only the sound of his name. Branimir's mission is to kill US President John Brown, the man who initiated war with many countries like Iran and Afghanistan and even Serbia (called Yugoslavia at that time) in the late 1990s. He's just waiting for a good moment to launch a nuclear attack on Russia.

This task makes Branimir extremely excited because he has a big personal beef with the US president. Of course, Connor used that information. It isn't confirmed, but it's suspected that a member of Branimir's family died from an explosion during the USA's bombing attacks in 1999. NATO launched its campaign without the UN's approval, stating that it was a humanitarian intervention.

Nala Onyejekwe is a South African beauty who wears a blue bandana as her trademark. She has dark, silky skin, a clean, beautiful face, and a lean body. She uses her beauty as a weapon of distraction, which gives her easier access to her targets during many of her missions. Her mission is to kill Egyptian terrorist leader Amir Mohammed, the most feared man in Africa. To the public, he's a powerful businessman; however, not many know how many murders per year in the entire African continent are committed according to his orders. He's building modern cities, factories, and roads, and he's killing everyone who stands in his way, especially the families who don't want to give up their land for modern projects.

Nicos Samaras, "The Greek man with a thousand faces," is the one responsible for spreading the Meng Virus that night in Guangzhou when he wore a black bunny gas mask. He's a master of disguise and has thousands of masks and costumes that he uses for his missions. His final mission is to kill the leaders of China, India, Pakistan, and Israel, who are all going to be in the same place at the same time. This will do a lot to stop the impending nuclear war.

Emilio Ruiz, originally from Malaga, Spain, was born and raised in Colombia. His shiny black hair is always slicked back "Italian style." Standing at medium height with dark eyebrows, he looks similar to Andy Garcia in the movie *Ocean's Twelve*. Known as the deadliest Nobody, he's a good friend of Connor's and the only Nobody who has ever seen Connor's face. Emilio has a record of 317 murders since he became a Nobody for Connor Emilio is famous for always getting the job done. His 317 murders say a lot about his success rate. Liam is the only person who has managed to escape from Emilio and even wound him, which still bugs Emilio at night. But Connor aborted that mission, for now. Emilio hasn't received a final mission yet. He's the ace up Connor's sleeve in case of emergency.

For all of them, their kills need to happen within five minutes before or after the times given to them. This means that due to time differences between the various continents and countries, all the targets should be killed at approximately the same time.

Country leaders, cartel leaders, terrorist leaders, all of them know that New Year's Eve is the best night for a secret meeting because the entire world's focus will be on celebrating the beginning of a new decade.

Except Connor, who is always few steps ahead of everyone . . .

CHAPTER 39

I Choose Me

"No, no, no, no, no!" Liam shouts . "Who the hell do they think they are?" He's furious.

"Hey, calm down," Alice says. "We need to talk about this."

"There isn't anything to talk about. This is madness!" He walks in a circle while scratching his head with both hands.

Alice watches him pace. "Madness? Why? Are the two of you related? Is he someone important in your life?"

Liam stops and stares at her. "He's the fucking president of France!"

Alice's task is to kill the president of France, but Liam is to participate by helping her access him.

"I know! Did you not read it clearly? There's something bigger behind all of this."

"Bigger? Says who? The person behind the game app? Do we even know it's a real person? Fucking bullshit. I'm going to report this!" He looks around for his phone.

"You report this, and we're both dead, and the president will still be killed by someone else. Trust me!" She knows the power of The Nobodies.

"Why are we so scared of them?" he asks.

"Hey! Bigshot! Wake up!" She claps her hands. "I choose my life over anybody else's. President, king, I don't care. Like they care if I live or die, right? What would your dear president do if I died right now? He doesn't even know I exist. Fuck them all! It's about survival!"

Liam looks at her without saying anything, then shakes his head. "I can't do this. I can't betray my country. Anything else. Anything." He looks defeated.

"What if he's right?" Alice asks. "Whoever he is doesn't matter. What if he's right, and your president is working with Oliver, son of the English Prince Richard, on a nuclear attack on China and Russia? Helping kill him wouldn't be betraying your country. You would be saving millions of lives."

That actually works. Liam begins thinking about it. "Recently, there have been a lot of visits from Oliver, son of Prince Richard, to France and meetings with our president. When I think about it, President Caron has been visiting England more than usual as well. But that would be the end of the world as we know it. It would be the biggest disaster ever recorded. Nuclear bombs, billions would be burned alive if that person is right, but if not, it would just be us murdering the president. Not to mention, how the hell could we do that?"

"Well, they send us his movement and everything in detail. That's what The Nobodies are all about, getting us information so precise so that even a child can murder an important person with some detailed planning."

"But Alice, they're asking us to kill him in his home on New Year's Eve. It's cruel. This is a nightmare." He shakes his head at the thought.

"It's definitely not perfect," Alice admits, "but I would do anything to be out of that organization, and I will not pass up this opportunity. I don't enjoy killing, but my life right now leads me to make some choices that many other people never have to."

"How can you be so calm?" Liam asks. "It seems like this is so natural to you. You're very cold about this, like it isn't a matter of human lives." He shakes his head in confusion. "I don't know if you're still that sweet, lovely girl that I fell in love with or a cold-blooded killer."

"I'm both ," Alice says, taking up a paper and pen. Shall we?"

CHAPTER 40

Let's Kill A Prince

"Do you think it's doable?" Bogdan asks. He and Victor are in Bogdan's motel room after receiving their task through the app.

"Well, they gave us a lot of details on his movement, location, etcetera," Victor replies. "If it's all correct, as always, we should be able to do it." Despite his words, he looks concerned.

"But?" Bogdan sighs .

"After we do it, it's nearly impossible to get away from his property. It's an island. I don't see any options so far." His eyes narrow as he thinks about it.

"There's a lot of security members for a New Year's Eve dinner for friends and family," Bogdan says. "I guess his conscience isn't that clear." He reads the details from the app again.

"Where are The Nobodies getting all of this information?" Victor asks. "How do these people know about the nuclear war that's apparently on the way? How is it possible that of all the special forces, mercenaries, and private armies, the two of us are the ones to get involved with this? This is insane." He shakes his head at the thought.

"Sometimes the more I think, the more lost I get," Bogdan admits. "So now I just want to get this mission over with and leave all of this behind." He stands up.

Victor stands up as well. "You're right. I've been too emotional about this. Let's work on the plan. It needs to be perfect. It's not every day we get to kill the son of the Prince of England."

CHAPTER 41

New Year's Eve

The entire world is celebrating. People are saying goodbye to one decade and welcoming a brand-new one. Everyone is praying and wishing that the decade will bring them something good—more money, more health, more of everything that's good and less of everything that's bad.

For the Nobodies, this is the night where they can free themselves. No more looking over their shoulders. No more being suspicious of every person who tries to get close to them or even speak with them, but there's a big mountain to climb before that becomes a reality.

At 9:00 p.m., Connor opens the door of his house, and Vera walks in with a bottle of champagne.

"Didn't you tell me that champagne for you is like a grape juice after the rivers of vodka that you've drank?" Connor asks, smiling.

"I can drink grape juice for some special occasions," she replies, returning the smile.

"Come in, please. Welcome. Let me take your coat."

"Thank you." Vera looks around. It's all the same as when she visited a couple of years earlier. Vera is always blown away that there is no security. It looks like a regular home. No one is looking for Connor. He's just a regular guy in this world. No one knows the truth.

After a few glasses of champagne, they get into a deep conversation.

"You know, I need to ask, are you the one responsible for that Meng Virus in China and India?" Connor nods. "You're cutting the population?" she asks calmly.

Connor nods again. "Yes." The only person he can actually talk about it with is Vera. Maybe that's why he called her. He needs to talk about it with someone.

"But it's going to affect many innocent people, isn't it? I see that you made a virus for only those two nations somehow." She knows that Connor's mind is made up, so there's no point trying to change his opinion, but she's curious about his answer.

"I'm not sure anymore what makes people innocent. But yes, many will die so many more can live a happier life in the future and extend the life of this dying planet." There is no sign of regret on his face.

"How come you care so much about the future?" Vera asks. "Forgive me for saying this, but you don't even have children. For whom do you want to provide that nice future?" She's asking in a natural and friendly way. He knows she will not use his answer against him or judge him. OK, maybe she'll judge him a bit.

Connor looks at her for a moment. It's an innocent look followed by a brief smile. "All of this looks—and probably is—crazy, but if there's one thing that makes me upset in this world, it's the same reason that this planet will eventually fail: human selfishness. We build cities, planes, satellites, and spaceships, but we can't learn one thing about being kind and respecting one another or respecting nature. Look at the animals around the world. For the past billion years, what has changed in their lives? Nothing! Billions of years, and they still hunt, eat, sleep, play, reproduce, and enjoy their family members. They don't need spaceships, artificial intelligence, or nuclear weapons. You know that the biggest threat for all living beings on this, the only planet we have, are humans. We established that a few weeks ago. So yes, if you tell me innocent people will die from my virus, I ask you, who really is innocent? And why are we so important over other living creatures and even nature itself?" He's a bit upset, but he calms down quickly.

"You're one of a kind; that's for sure," Vera says. Connor regards her for a moment to see if she's being sarcastic.

"From nothing, you made a great fortune for yourself, by yourself," Vera continues. "I don't even know how, but I won't ask. You can do anything, and yet you chose to do what you do. I've never heard you say anything about getting rich, fast cars, business, women, yachts, everything that would normally interest rich people. Instead, you've invested everything you have in trying to make this planet a better place for billions of people. Not through charities and other bullshit but by cleaning up other people's messes, rolling up your sleeves, and doing what's necessary. Even though sometimes it's cruel, it's for the greater good. The Human God. That's what you've always been to me. The Human God."

Connor feels emotional. He's breathing deeply, his eyes teary. Her respect goes directly to his heart. She hit the spot.

"Thank you," he says. "But I don't believe in God. More champagne?" He stands up to get another bottle.

Meanwhile, just before 6:00 p.m. in Colombia

Klaus is putting the pilot's helmet on his head inside a Lockheed Martin F-35 Lightning II airplane at a small, hidden private airport. It's an all-weather, stealth, multi-role combat aircraft designed for air superiority and strike missions. The F-35 is better than any other fighter aircraft, including the F-22, for air-to-ground strike missions. Klaus has six missiles and is planning to drop one on the villa, one on each of the three huge hangars, and two on the drug fields. The ensuing fire will take care of the rest.

Inside the villa, Esteban Rojo is raising a glass and giving a welcome speech about family and partnership with all other Latin cartel leaders, who nod when Esteban reviews statistics of the billions of dollars that they made together over the previous decade.

"Salud mi familia!" he says in conclusion, finishing his speech at exactly 6:00 p.m. Everyone is taking a sip of champagne when the heat of the explosion tears them to pieces, together with the entire villa.

Klaus releases all his missiles, and everything is burning in that small, hidden area of Colombia—the villa, the hangars, the fields, and the security guards. Security was high for the event, but they never expected an aerial attack.

The F-35 vanishes into the sky, leaving nothing behind but fire and ashes.

At approximately the same time in Russia

Nathan is already in the building. He needs to sneak past a few security guards.

Russian Prime Minister Kiril Smirnov is planning to poison Russian President Popov at the end of the midnight toast that has just finished and is on his way to a private bar to pour two last glasses of champagne for both of them.

Kiril looks around and sees only one member of President Popov's security detail inside the room with them and a few outside the door. President Popov is a good man. He sent most of his security guards home to celebrate New Year's Eve with their families.

Kiril pours poisonous powder into President Popov's glass, mixes it, and then walks slowly toward him.

Nathan is aiming through the balcony window. The second before he pulls the trigger, he feels cold metal on the back of his head.

"Drop the gun!" says a man with a strong Russian accent.

Nathan is instantly covered in sweat as he runs through his options. He can't come up with any, so he drops his gun.

The security guard knocks on the balcony door, and the other guard who's in the room pulls out a gun and approaches the door.

What the fuck is that? Kiril wonders. He's extremely confused seeing Nathan in a uniform with no flag patch on it.

Nathan looks at President Popov. "Mr. President, don't drink that champagne! Your 'friend' is trying to poison you to start World War Three with the USA, a nuclear war!"

The others in the room look at him in confusion.

"Who are you?" President Popov asks. "Do you have proof of what you're saying?"

"Yes, the poison in that glass and the USB in my left pocket." The USB is the coverage if he got caught in case the Russian president thought that Nathan had been sent to kill him.

Before the president can reply, two bullets hit Nathan in the chest. While everyone else was focused on Nathan, Kiril pulled out his gun and shot him. Kiril can't afford to be discovered. They will execute him in the blink of an eye.

Pushed back by the bullets hitting his chest but protected by his bulletproof vest, Nathan disarms a security guard and shoots the prime minister three times—two times in the chest and one time on the side of the head above his ear. Then he feels a strong impact on his neck as the second security guard shoots him, and Nathan falls dead.

"Why did you do that?" President Popov yells at the security guard who shot Nathan.

"Sir, he killed the prime minister!"

The president looks at Kiril's body. "Search the intruder's uniform for the USB, and don't approach where the champagne is spilled. Call the FSB. I want the champagne searched for any poisonous substance."

He knows his security guard acted instinctively and probably correctly, but he is sorry if Nathan is right. He didn't deserve to die.

At approximately the same time in the Arabian Sea

While boarding a yacht earlier that day, Nicos was searched by security. He had his face painted to look like a clown, including a round red nose and a curly multi-colored wig. Other than that he was in normal clothes.

Nicos gave two of his suitcases, which look funny and have clowns and circus stickers on them, to some kids and promised to tell them a big secret if they put them in his room.

As the kids ran onto the yacht with his bags, Nicos waved to security to stop them but waited until the kids were already inside and out of the reach of security.

He pretended that they stole his bags while he was telling them a story before boarding the boat.

"Oh, those kids, they have no respect for an old clown," Nicos said. "They ran away with my bags. I'll catch them inside." The security guards asked what was in the bags because they didn't plan to chase the president's kids. "Nothing special," Nicos replied. "My costume and some toys for tonight's show. I'll find them on board. They don't have anywhere to hide." He was pretending he was already in his clown role.

They searched Nicos thoroughly and found nothing and didn't pay much attention to him in general or his bags. They had other things to worry about, such as keeping four presidents safe.

They're on a 126-meter mega yacht named *The Pearl* that's owned by the president of India. Around sixty crewmembers and twenty elite guests are waiting for midnight, which is just a few minutes away.

The presidents of China, India, Israel, and Pakistan are doing a special toast, five minutes before midnight, in a separate luxurious room, in order to celebrate the upcoming decade and the new alliance between their countries in the upcoming nuclear attack planned against the USA, which they finalized a few days earlier.

Their special ladies are also present, competing over which one spent more during the previous decade.

Outside on the second floor of the yacht, their children are enjoying the performance of a clown hired to keep them entertained. The rich kids are making fun of the clown, and some are throwing snacks at him, which made them laugh even more.

The clown doesn't mind; he's expecting all of this. It's 11:55 p.m., and Nicos has just finished his performance and let the kids know that's it for today and that he will just to use the bathroom to refresh himself and then take them to their moms.

Nicos walks slowly toward the bathroom. He looks fat under his costume and is sweating profusely. The bathroom is on his right, but he continues walking straight until he reaches the hallway on the first floor.

Nicos unzips his jacket and pulls out a silenced M4 carbine assault rifle and looks down the left hallway, where two bodyguards stand in front of a door. The hallway isn't very long, so he's able to shoot them both before they even realize what's happening.

Nicos reaches under his jacket again and grabs a flash grenade. He opens the door slightly and throws it into the room.

After the grenade goes off, he enters the room and eliminates two other bodyguards, who were stunned by the grenade. He looks around and sees no one except four presidents holding their ears and faces in shock at the flashbang's stunning effect.

He thinks for a moment about how pathetic they look, rolling on the floor, panting, the same group of men who plan to take millions of lives in a nuclear war.

Nicos shoots the Pakistani president first because he seems to be the least affected by the flashbang. He kills the Chinese and Israeli presidents, then stands in front of the Indian president.

"Wait, wait, I'll give you anything you want!" the man pleads.

"What I want is to kill you," Nicos says, firing two bullets into the Indian president's face.

Nicos removes the clown costume, and while everyone else is preparing for the midnight toast, which is three minutes away, he uses the rope that's wrapped around him to slide through the window directly to the water.

He looked fat in the clown costume earlier because he was wearing a wetsuit, oxygen tank, rifle, flash grenade, rope, and a few other things under the costume, which also made him heavier and made him sweat a lot.

Nearby is a small inflatable boat with a silent outboard motor, sent to follow the yacht while maintaining a three-hundred-meter distance.

Distracted by the fireworks display, everyone is looking up instead of at the water. However, Nicos still swims underwater just in case someone looks down and happens to spot him.

"Happy New Year, Nicos," he says to himself as he surfaces and bobs in the water. "You're a free clown now." His eyes fill with tears of happiness, knowing he has completed his last mission.

At approximately the same time in Egypt

Nala is standing in front of one of the biggest villas she has ever seen. Her target, Amir, is throwing a New Year's Eve party similar to the one in Colombia that his friend Esteban Rojo is throwing, but this one is more open and much bigger.

Amir is known in public as a successful businessman, so he doesn't need to hide from anyone. His life as a terrorist leader is so well hidden that not even his family knows the truth.

Tonight he welcomes all his biggest partners and their families and even their cousins and "plus ones." More than a hundred people are inside the villa.

Nala is dressed like a man in tuxedo with a black ribbon under her chin. She's not wearing any makeup, her hair is hidden under her hat, and she's wearing a fake mustache. She easily passes through the security because The Nobodies got her name on the guest list. Tonight she's Mr. Elimu Adisa, a "plus one" of one of Amir's cousins.

Nala arrives an hour early to get to know the villa better and to prepare. She knows how to walk, talk, and behave like a man. She practiced for a week, five hours a day, like she was preparing for a movie role.

It's 11:53 p.m. when Nala enters the men's washroom. She checks around to make sure no one is there. Then she goes inside one of the stalls and removes her clothes, hat, mustache, and places it all in the toilet tank—everything except her hat, which she throws out the window.

She's wearing a pink miniskirt and a short white shirt that reveals her sexy stomach. Her hair falls over her shoulders, and she looks nothing like she did a few seconds earlier.

Nala also has a small silenced gun strapped to her leg. Amir doesn't want anyone to be searched by security. He doesn't want to insult any of his guests on this gala-night.

At 11:55 p.m., Amir enters the same washroom to take a leak. After nearly fifty minutes of his midnight speech for over a hundred people, his bladder wants to explode. The Nobodies know about his overactive bladder. He needs to urinate more often than a regular person, especially after a long speech like that.

It's a small, insignificant problem, Amir thinks. He pees a lot, especially when he drinks alcohol. It's not a big deal; many people do. He has no idea that tonight it will cost him his life.

The moment Amir pulls out his dick and turns his back to the toilet stalls, Nala fires a bullet into the back of his head, and he falls to the floor, dead.

Nala turns around and places the gun inside of the toilet tank and then closes it. Then she goes to the entrance and screams as loud as she can.

A member of Amir's security detail enters immediately and sees his boss's dead body. Nala is still screaming.

"Hey, hey, what happened here?" the guard asks, holding her by the shoulders and shaking her. "Tell me!"

"The guy . . . the guy with the hat . . . He pulled out a gun. Oh my god, oh my god . . ." She pretends to be hysterical.

"Where is he now?" the guard asks, losing patience. "Tell me!"

"He jumped!" She points to the window above the toilet. "He jumped!"

The security guard runs and looks out the window, noticing the black hat on the grass. He looks left and right but doesn't see anyone, though he knows the man can't be far. He turns back to Nala. "Miss, what's he wearing?" But she's already gone, having left the bathroom and mixed in with the hundreds of people who are still unaware that their host is dead.

The security guard prioritizes the pursuit of the "killer" and jumps through the window, picking up the hat. Then he alerts all the other security guards.

Nala is already off the property, swallowed by the dark night that's brightened from time to time as huge fireworks explode in all directions, announcing the arrival of the new decade.

At approximately 11:55 p.m. in England.

North Korean Supreme Leader Min-Jun is celebrating New Year's Eve with his family in his big house next to the lake in a place called Heaton in England. Min-Jun purchased the house many years ago, and it's a perfect getaway for such special occasions.

He has some security outside but not many. He sent most of them home to celebrate with their families. Min-Jun's spouse, his three sons, and one sister are there, and that's about it.

Luca Rosso doesn't have a very difficult task . He has to go in, kill the supreme leader, then escape into the forest.

Luca does not want to kill any of the security guards as part of his plan, but he's ready to do so if they interfere. There are only three of them, and they are all outside.

It's midnight, and fireworks go off around the country. Min-Jun and his entire family have gone outside to shoot off some of their own.

Min-Jun finishes a glass of champagne and is setting the empty champagne flute on the table when he feels a strong pain first in his jaw and then in his forehead as bullets crash into his skull.

Luca notices Min-Jun's ten year-old son, Ming, looking at him with teary eyes before Luca runs away into the forest and vanishes for good.

Luca knows those teary eyes will haunt him forever.

Every time he blinks, he will see ten-year-old Ming standing next to his dead father with a devastated look on his face.

At approximately 4:00 p.m. in Washington, DC

US President John Brown and his family are having the time of their lives inside the White House where the family has lived for four years.

His eldest son, William, who is sixteen years old, reminds him of their tradition of firing fireworks from the rooftop at midnight, but they always go up at around 4:00 p.m. to set everything up, so when they go on the roof at midnight, they only need to light it up.

"How could I forget that?" John asks. "We must respect tradition!" He's also excited about it.

"Let's go, Dad," William says later that evening. "It's almost midnight. Everything is already on the roof. Hurry up!"

The captain of the White House security detail nods to the president as they check to ensure the area is safe.

They do it every year because around the White House there isn't anything taller than a house. No huge business buildings, nothing, because the most logical concern is a sniper attack on the president. This is the fifth year that they are respecting the tradition set by William.

The fireworks are set up mainly by William and his brother. John helps them occasionally but wants to see if they know how to do it on their own after he showed them how to do it during the previous few years.

William notices a hot-air balloon in the sky and points it out to his father. "Look, a hot-air balloon, Dad! How cool! And it has an American flag on it! Happy New Year!" He waves in the balloon's direction.

"Yes, cool," the president says. "Hmm . . . it's blue, red, and white, but I don't think it's our flag." He approaches the edge of the balcony for a closer look. "I think it's the Serbian flag." As he says those words, he frowns, remembering that he bombarded Serbia twenty years earlier.

He sees a flash coming from the hot-air balloon basket, like someone is using a digital camera, but a second later, he feels unbearable pain as a huge bullet from a sniper goes through his lungs.

The US president falls onto his back, coughing blood. He dies in seconds before anyone becomes aware of what's happening.

Branimir jumps out of the hot-air balloon and slides down a rope tied to the basket. All his stuff is in the balloon, which is now flying on its own.

Some people on the street notice him slide down the rope, but they have no idea that he just shot the president.

Branimir unlocks his car, which is parked just a few meters away, gets inside, pulls a picture of a young girl from his pocket, and focuses on it for a second. "Now you can rest in peace, my princess."

At approximately the same time in France.

Every year at 8:00 p.m., the president of France addresses the nation on TV with a presidential greeting "Les vœux présidentiels." The speech is broadcast from the Élysée Palace, the official residence of the French president and the French equivalent of the White House. During this presidential greeting, the president takes stock of the past year and expresses his political vision and his wishes for the future of France.

Liam uses his connections to place Alice on the small Bonjour-TV crew, which is made of only four people. That's the only thing that The Nobodies requested of him. Alice is in charge of makeup, which she's very familiar with, having tried and promoted some smaller makeup brands on her Instagram page.

At 7:50 p.m., President Thierry Caron walks into the room and sits on a chair behind a big wooden desk. He's young with short black hair, a regular-looking guy.

Alice observes for a second and then walks toward President Caron, but a big black security guard steps in front of her.

"I need to check your bag, Miss," he says, his face serious.

"Oh, your colleague already did that outside and . . . Right, never mind, sorry, you need to check. It's protocol." President Caron finds that funny. The security guard checks her makeup bag quickly and then lets her pass.

"Do I need a lot of makeup or will a bit do?" President Caron asks. He isn't married, and he's prone to flirting, but he's very careful where he does it. He's in his home, so he feels safe.

"Just a bit will do," Alice says. She's happy she caught his eye. She might be able to manipulate the situation better.

One of his security guards approaches, places a champagne flute in front of the president, and pours champagne into it.

"Have you been in this business for a long time?" President Caron asks.

"It's been a few years, yeah," she says as she applies foundation to his face.

"You're not French . . . Australian?" He's familiar with the accent.

"Is it that obvious?" she asks as she continues "fixing" his face.

"It's one of my favorite accents," he says quietly, almost whispering.

Alice opens her eyes as wide as she can and places her face in front of his, checking if the makeup is done. The president finds this quite amusing. Her big blue eyes a hypnotic. Not many men are immune to them.

She turns around to reach into her makeup bag, which is on the president's desk next to his champagne flute, and the president uses the moment to check out Alice from behind. *Great body,* he thinks.

Alice's job is done, so she turns around and waves to the president before she goes behind the camera, and filming begins.

No one notices that Alice sprayed a touch of Vitolicerin 12 into the president's champagne flute, especially not President Caron, who was too busy checking out Alice's butt at the time. If he drinks it now, the poison should kick in at around midnight.

President Caron gives his speech, wishing all the best to the entire country and sharing his hopes that the next decade will be even better.

Close to the end, he reaches for his champagne flute. He accidentally knocks it over, and the glass breaks, spilling champagne all over the desk.

Fuck no! Alice screams to herself.

"This is my first glass of champagne," President Caron jokes, "I promise!" He smiles and makes a few jokes about it, then motions for his security guard to bring him another one.

Alice almost goes to do it herself, but she can't; it's a live program. Inside her head, she's panicking.

The president drinks a brand-new glass of champagne and wishes everyone happy holidays.

When the speech is done, the president leaves the room immediately together with the majority of his security detail.

I'm so fucked! Alice thinks. She's terrified. She failed.

"Come on, girl," one of the other crewmembers says. "Let's go. Are you deaf?" They have already packed up and are about to leave the room.

The entire Bonjour-TV crew is at the exit when one of the security guards pulls Alice aside. "Go out of the house, and make sure your crew thinks you left to go home, then come back and knock," he says. "I'll let you in. President Caron wants to see you."

Alice is in shock, but she realizes this is her chance, the last one ever, and she better not fuck it up.

She follows the instructions, and after the TV crew leaves, the security guard escorts her to the president's room and leaves her in front of the door. "The president is expecting you," he says, motioning for her to enter.

Alice opens the door and finds President Caron sitting in a leather chair.

"I would regret forever if I let you go home," he says, smiling.

"I can stay for a bit," Alice says. She knows she needs to buy some time. The Nobodies are very specific that the kill needs to happen at around 1:00 a.m.

"A bit?" He stands up. "Oh, come on, you can do better than that."

"That depends," Alice says. She continues to play hard to get and walks over to the window and looks out. They're on the ground floor.

"Aha, I get it," President Caron says. "You like to play games. I like to think that I'm a player myself." He has a confident smile that doesn't work at all on Alice.

"What does a girl need to do around here to be offered a beverage?" she asks. She tries to stay away from any physical interaction for as long as possible.

"What do you like?" he asks. President Caron helps her to hang her coat on the hanger next to the door and then walks her into the room.

"Hmm . . . let me see, I'm in the president's house, so surprise me." She sits in the leather chair and crosses her shiny, smooth legs.

Alice is wearing a light-blue long-sleeve shirt that matches her eyes and a grey skirt that goes down to her knees.

For the next few hours, they chat and drink, though Alice tries not to drink too much.

At midnight, President Caron kisses Alice's neck, moving all the way up to her lips. "Happy New Year, sexy!" he says.

Alice forces a smile. "Happy New Year. Would you mind if I use your bathroom to take quick shower? I've been working all day." She needs to buy at least one more hour, or close to that.

"Of course, but hurry," Caron says. "I miss you already." At this point, he's already a bit tipsy. "But wait, can you put this on after you shower?" He opens a cupboard and pulls out a "slutty police uniform." He has a cupboard full of such things that he gets girls to wear during sex.

Alice smiles. "Sure, love. I recommend you place a 'Do Not Disturb' sign on the door. It's going to be a long, wild night."

She goes into the bathroom and takes her sweet time inside while President Caron calls his security team to let them know not to disturb them and to go and have a party of their own with the rest of the house staff in one of the empty rooms.

It's 12:30 a.m. when Alice comes out of the bathroom wearing the slutty police uniform.

"Oh, baby, I was a very bad boy, just so you know!" He's losing his mind as he watches Alice walk toward him, spinning the cuffs on her index finger.

"How bad?" Alice asks, smiling wickedly.

"Very, very bad!"

She approaches slowly and cuffs him to the bed. He tries to kiss her, but she lifts her lips and allows him to kiss her all over the neck instead. "I don't kiss bad boys," Alice says. "I fuck them."

President Caron wants to explode. She starts rubbing herself on his leg. Alice looks at the clock. It's 12:50 a.m.

Slowly, she removes his underwear. Then Thierry starts coughing and shaking. Foam starts coming out of his mouth, and Alice steps away from him and runs to the bathroom to wash her neck, which she sprayed with Vitolicerin 12.

When she returns, he's already white, cold, and dead.

Alice dresses in her clothes, opens the window, and sneaks out into the night.

At approximately the same time on the Isle of Man, Ireland

Prince Oliver, son of Prince Richard, the only son of the queen of England, has rented a huge castle on the Isle of Man to hold a New Year's Eve party for his friends and business partners.

The ferry takes up to two hours and forty-five minutes to reach the island from Liverpool, but Prince Oliver rented a big yacht to transport all of his guests, who are coming from England or through England.

Prince Oliver is playing a big part in the nuclear war that's about to start the following year but, he's also planning the execution of his grandmother, the queen, and his father, who is next in line for the crown. With them gone, he will be the first in line to rule.

Before any of the guests arrive, a big catering company called the Golden Fork arrives to set up the event. They are in charge of providing guests with a buffet dinner and setting up open bars full of alcohol for them to enjoy.

Victor, who is a restaurant manager back in Canada, managed to get hired under a different name for the event as a part-time server. His experience is excellent, and the company desperately needs more "elite servers" for the event.

Victor is setting the tables and placing tablecloths on them, but one eye is always looking elsewhere. *Lots of security,* he thinks, *like The Nobodies said it would be* .

It's 8:00 p.m. when the guests start to arrive. The guards search them for any weapons and then check them in using a computer tablet.

Bogdan shows up with a beautiful lady on his arm. The Nobodies requested two assassins for this mission in case one of them fails because the security level is so high. Bogdan is unrecognizable with fake brown hair and glasses. He's wearing a black suit with a grey shirt underneath. His escort, a lady he hired earlier to be his plus one for the event, is in a beautiful red dress.

"Name please, sir," a security guard says.

"Mr. Tom Parker," Bogdan smiled .

"Found it. Mr. Parker. Your accent sounds Russian," the guard says.

Bogdan nods. "Yes, from my mother's side." He smiles and walks into the castle's huge yard.

Bogdan and Helena, the name of his escort, walk around, trying to stay away from anyone and not to get involved in any long conversations. She's been instructed to avoid even small chats. Helena only met Bogdan when he was already masked and introduced to her as Tom Parker, and she has no idea of his intentions.

Victor makes sure that he's the guy who goes around with a bottle of red and a bottle of white wine and fills the guest's glasses, which gives him access to everyone at the party.

"Helena, please go to the washroom," Bogdan says. "Take five minutes, and then come back to me, OK?" Helena nods and then leaves.

Victor notices that and approaches Bogdan. "Would you prefer red or white wine, sir?"

"Red would be great. Did you manage to find the gun?" Bogdan whispers as Victor starts to pour.

Victor nods to confirm that he did and then approaches the other guests nearby. "More wine for you, madam?"

Bogdan and Victor arrived at the Isle of Man the day before as tourists and buried a few guns around the island, near the castle.

After he was searched and dressed in his black-and-white server's uniform earlier, Victor went to the garden and dug out a small pistol with a silencer and strapped it to his ankle.

The party progresses as expected. People are getting increasingly drunk, the buffet is getting hit hard, and DJ Remix starts playing his beats at 11:30 p.m. He has an amazing setup with huge speakers and multi-colored disco lights cutting through the night.

Meanwhile, Bogdan manages to dig up one of the guns for himself and straps it to his right leg as Victor did a few hours earlier.

A few minutes before midnight, DJ Remix speaks into his microphone. "Five minutes left, party people!"

Bogdan looks at Victor one more time and then leaves the party.

Security stops him for a moment "Leaving, sir?"

"Silly me," Bogdan says. "I forgot a special gift for Mr. Oliver on my yacht. It's moored nearby. I'll be back in a minute." He hurries away from the party.

Everyone is at the bar getting a drink for the midnight toast, and a lot of people are dancing and jumping around. People are acting wild, and some of them are already falling on the grass and rolling around, drunk, and careless.

"Ten, nine, eight . . ." DJ Remix screams into the microphone.

Victor recognizes the moment and walks directly into the crowd. He pulls out his gun and places it under the server's jacket, under his armpit, while in his other hand he holds a bottle of champagne.

DJ Remix continues the countdown. "Four, three . . ."

At that moment Victor passes in front of the Prince Oliver, fires a bullet into his heart, then drops the gun in another guest's jacket pocket and continues walking through the crowd with only the bottle of champagne in his hand.

"Two, one, Happy New Year!" DJ Remix shouts . He cranks the volume on the music, and the bass starts to pound.

No one notices as Prince Oliver falls to the ground because so many other drunkards are jumping, falling, and lying on the ground.

Victor is close to the exit gate that's a short distance from the main lawn where the party is being held and is guarded by four security guards when he hears the music stop and a woman scream.

All four security guards are alerted. "What's that?" one asks as they look toward the lawn. Victor is now in front of them.

"You guys at the door," a voice says over their radios. "Don't let anyone in or out. We've had a shooting here on the lawn."

They look at Victor. "Where do you think you're going, sir?" They eye him suspiciously.

"There was a shooting there. I don't want to die!" he says, acting scared.

They are all looking at Victor when Bogdan comes up from behind and shoots them one by one. Bogdan manages to kill only two of them as they are wearing bulletproof vests, and he has to shoot them in the head as the other two manage to pull out their guns.

Victor jumps on one of them from behind and takes him to the ground, causing the guard to drop his gun.

The other security guard who's still standing exchanges fire with Bogdan, who is shot twice in his left leg before he shoots the security guard in the forehead.

Victor is still lying on the ground with his arm around the last security guard's neck. He holds him until he chokes to death.

Victor stands up and sees Bogdan grimacing in pain as he tries to stop the bleeding from two bullet holes in his left leg. Victor helps him up, and he runs as fast as he can with Bogdan on his back toward their small yacht, which is tied up nearby.

What buys them a lot of time is that security searches the guests close to Prince Oliver's body and finds the gun that

Victor dropped in the jacket pocket of one of the guests, who turns out to be a corrupt cop working for Prince Oliver. He's the main suspect at the moment, and that moment is enough for Victor and Bogdan to leave the island on their small yacht, called *The Jellyfish*.

Meanwhile at Connor's house . . .

For a few hours, Vera and Connor go over some events and missions and many other things that connect the two of them. Vera doesn't know when they'll meet again, so she decides to ask the question that's been burning in her mind. "I don't want to spoil the moment, but I want to know more about your 'big project,' you know, the one that made you leave the three of us after so many years of partnership. Is there more to it, or is it just that virus and the situation with the poachers a few months ago?"

"Well," Connor says, knowing he can trust her. "Let's turn on the TV. Everything will be clear in a few minutes." He smiles at Vera's confusion. "I had one of my guys, the best hacker in the world, pay Natalie Archer big bucks to read a letter I wrote on live TV tonight at five minutes after midnight." He grabs a remote and turns on the TV. It's a few moments before midnight. Connor turns the channel to WNC, which always shares the latest international news.

A few minutes later, Vera looks at the clock. It's midnight. "Happy New Year, my friend!"

Connor smiles "Happy New Decade, my forever friend!" He hugs her.

On TV, the stunning green-eyed redhead Natalie Archer wishes everyone a Happy New Year. She stops for a moment as one of her assistants delivers an envelope to her.

"Ladies and gentlemen, it looks like we have some big updates even on New Year's Eve!" She opens the envelope and pulls out a letter.

Connor looks at Vera. "This is it! It's finally happening!" Connor's heart is beating fast as Natalie starts reading.

"To get your attention in the first place, I want to say that I'm the one responsible for creating the Meng Virus and also for the Poachers' Massacre in Zimbabwe," Natalie says. "Tonight, on New Year's Eve, my people eliminated the president of France, the president of China, the president of Pakistan, the president of India, the president of Israel, the president of the United States, the prime minister of Russia, and Prince Oliver of the United Kingdom." She stops for a moment and looks at the camera. At the same moment, Vera looks Connor, who is focused on what Natalie is saying.

"Yes, you heard it correctly. I've also eliminated the biggest drug cartel families in Latin America and the biggest terrorist in Africa, Amir Muhammed. The news will come shortly all over the world after my letter is read.

"No matter what I say in my defense, I will still be labeled as a criminal and the number-one target of all governments and criminals around the world, but I will still say it.

"The gentlemen that I mentioned above are all planning a nuclear war in the new year. The USA, France, and the UK against Russia, China, Pakistan, India, and Israel. Many proofs have been saved, but I have sent some on the USB together with this letter."

Vera looks at Connor. *Is this real?* she wonders. This is huge, even for him.

"Lastly, as bizarre as it sounds, I've created a hybrid mosquito, that will eliminate all the regular mosquitos all over the world, which cause over seven hundred and fifty thousand deaths each year. But before you thank me, know this. The 'Angel Mosquitos,' as I call them, are deadlier than regular mosquitos, but only if you're a drug user, a smoker, an alcoholic, or you have a deadly transmittable disease. They will bite, and their bite will kill you in a few days. Angel Mosquitos are completely harmless to the people unless you're doing one of the above things. You have been warned."

Vera can't believe what she's hearing.

"All of you must be wondering what I want," Natalie continues, "so I'll tell you. First, I want the human mentality to change. I want us to stop being selfish and careless about this planet, nature, animals, and even ourselves. I want poor people to stop only thinking about getting rich and rich people to stop thinking about how to get richer. I will leave it to you to come up with a solution for how everyone can be on the same level.

"I've become disgusted and tired of seeing the behavior of people around the world. For me, humans are the biggest enemy of humanity, nature, animals, and this planet. It has to stop now."

"Second is a message for all governments. I want all nuclear weapons to be disarmed and destroyed. Will investing billions in nuclear weapons will ever bring us anything good? The answer is no. You can have your armies, but no nuclear weapons. Let's invest those billions of dollars in something more beneficial for everyone, such as schools and hospitals.

"When these two conditions are accomplished, I will destroy my mosquitos, and I will deliver millions of vaccines for the Meng Virus. Until then, I'll be watching."

There's a moment of silence before the explosion of panic in all the studios around the world as news about the presidential assassinations starts to arrive.

Connor turns off the TV. He has instructed Tao Woo to send the Angel Mosquitos into the world in three days, so the entire world has time to hear the message.

The virus has already been out for two months.

All corrupt presidents are dead.

There isn't anything left for Connor to do except send cash and the message to all the remaining Nobodies, notifying them that they're free.

And then there's Vera. She's still looking at him, speechless. He smiles at her. "Albert Einstein once said 'The world will not be destroyed by those who do evil but by those who watch them without doing anything.'"

CHAPTER 42

Broken Dreams

After they kill Prince Oliver, Victor and Bogdan plan to go to Ireland on their yacht. However, after sailing for ten minutes, they are stopped by a big yacht named *Destiny*.

The people on *Destiny* explain that they have been sent by The Nobodies to help them sail directly to Canada and to provide medical help to Bogdan, who is bleeding badly. Victor and Bogdan are very confused because this has never happened before, but they are in no situation to negotiate because Bogdan needs help fast.

All four of them—Bogdan, Victor, Leo, and D—move to *Destiny*, and few crew members climb onboard *The Jellyfish* and follow the big yacht as it sails.

It turns out *Destiny*'s crew really is there to help them, first with Bodgan's wounds and second by dropping them off in Newfoundland, where they have parked Bogdan's RV. They moor *The Jellyfish* in the harbor.

Destiny and her crew sail off toward an unknown location, and Victor, Bogdan, Leo, and D set off for Victor's house in Vancouver. He has a feeling that Lucy will be waiting for him there because that's what The Nobodies promised. He is having a hard time not pressing the pedal to the floor because he misses her so much.

It will take them a week to reach Vancouver. The total driving time is around eighty hours. Only Victor can drive, and they have to stop often for the dogs to have a run and relieve themselves.

Victor basically drives for twelve hours a day. The RV is packed with supplies, so they have enough food and everything else they need. He tries to call the house every day, but there is no response.

Bogdan sleeps for most of the trip except when he's eating and when Victor is cleaning his wounds and changing his bandages.

After a week, they arrive at Victor's home in Vancouver, and Victor rushes into the house.

"Lucy!" he cries, going from room to room. "Lucy!" He can't wait to see her.

In the living room, two black bags are sitting next to the sofa. Victor checks inside, and, as usual upon the completion of a task, the bags are full of money.

He knows that one is for him and the other for Bogdan. He doesn't care much about that, though, as he continues to search for Lucy.

He walks into the bedroom and notices an envelope on the nightstand. It's from Lucy. He rips it open and reads it.

> I'm sorry that things have to end this way, but it's for the best. Now I realize that after all these years I didn't know who you really are and with whom I've been sharing my life. It's all been a facade.
>
> You're a smiling, happy, enthusiastic guy on the outside, but inside you're a cold-blooded killer.

Yes, they told me everything about you. They never hurt me, and they never made me write this letter. This is all me.

It's difficult being stuck in a hotel room for two months but not as difficult as finding out this truth. I'm more disappointed than angry, and yes, very scared to continue my life with you. I need to go far away from you, and please, in the name of the old days, don't search for me. I can't love what you are.

Victor can only hear his deep breathing from running through all the rooms searching find her, only to find this piece of paper, the last thing he'll ever get from Lucy.

CHAPTER 43

The Freedom Of The Nobodies

One month after New Year's Eve

Luca Rosso is sitting in a street restaurant in Pisa, Italy, enjoying a glass of wine, pizza, and the light breeze going through his silky brown hair. It's a feeling of freedom that he has missed over the years.

Working for The Nobodies took a lot from him, and he's truly done with it. Like the rest of them, Luca also received a bag full of money, some fake passports, and documents as a farewell from The Nobodies.

Sometimes, while enjoying moments like this, he can still see the teary eyes of Ming, Min-Jun's ten-year-old son, standing next to his father's dead body.

Cederberg is a small mountainous area in the region of the Western Cape province of South Africa. It's beautiful, with huge fields of the rooibos plant growing there. It's used to make rooibos tea or red tea, which is a high-quality tea that South Africa proudly exports all over the world.

Nala invested a small part of her money and bought these fields for her and her big family, and now they own a respectable business producing and selling Only Rooibos Tea all over the world.

She couldn't be happier and always stops for a moment to look around at her fields and her family and appreciate that moment of life, a moment of freedom.In the wide blue scenery of the Mediterranean Sea, a medium-size yacht floats with its engine off in that precious silence.

Nicos is sitting in the stern fishing. Something grabs his hook and yanks on his fishing rod. It pulls so strongly that it manages to unhook itself and swim away, causing Nicos to slip and fall onto his back.

He lies there for a moment looking at the seagulls flying over his boat. Then he starts laughing. Louder and louder.

That's the moment when Nicos realizes he's free again. In Serbia there is a place called Zlatibor. It has wonderful carpets of green grass, mountains, wildlife, everything Branimir has ever wanted. Branimir bought himself a big house with a big farm attached. He has cows, pigs, chickens, corn fields, wheat fields and his favorite, horses. He lives by himself, and he's constantly busy, milking the cows, planting seeds, and feeding the animals. Branimir enjoys every second of it.

Today, Branimir is riding his black female horse, called Karma, which always reminds him that everything is done. His daughter can rest in peace now, and he can live a normal, quiet life.

Somewhere in Germany, Klaus knows the real feeling of freedom while he flies his small blue plane, a Piper Pacer PA-20. It's a four-seat, strut-braced, high-wing light aircraft built by Piper Aircraft in the post-World War II period.

He's going nowhere, just flying through the air and doing some skilled acrobatic moves. It's the best possible way for Klaus to spend the rest of his days.

Not all the Nobodies are so lucky . . .

Not Alice Hill.

Alice's face is on every TV channel, her picture stuck to every store in every country. Radio stations mention her name more than anything else, even during music programs.

No one knows who organized the assassinations of all the presidents, but everyone knows who killed the French president. Her fingerprints are everywhere, and everyone saw her face on the security cameras.

No one knows yet where she is, but everyone knows she's the key to finding the man who organized the most horrifying killing spree in human history.

CHAPTER 44

The Numbers Are Going Up

One month later

Exactly 23,682 people in China are dead from the Meng Virus. The Chinese government has announced a state of emergency and social distancing, and staying at home is mandatory to prevent the virus from spreading. They are still not accepting Connor's conditions to destroy their nuclear weapons. Neither are any other countries that possess nuclear weapons.

The Chinese president is dead, but they still believe they can find who ordered the assassination and avoid destroying their nuclear weapons, which are worth billions of dollars.

In India, 18,312 people are dead from the virus. India is following China's example. They have their most elite detectives searching for Connor across the entire world.

The rest of the world has finally seen the Angel Mosquitos. They are still multiplying, so there aren't many deaths yet, "just" 2,472 recorded deaths so far on the entire planet. Nothing that will make governments fulfill Connor's requests.

The USA, China, India, Pakistan, the UK, France, and Israel are hungry for revenge. Everyone except Russia. The Russian president is grateful that his life was saved, and even though he doesn't want to admit it, he secretly admires what Connor planned and executed. He finds it to be extraordinary.

A single man with the smallest "army" has basically defeated some of the most powerful countries in the world in five minutes.

CHAPTER 45

A "True Friend"

Somewhere in France

Liam is standing in the rain and looking at his watch. It's 10:00 p.m., and no one is on the streets. He looks around as a cold breeze crawls up under his coat.

Someone walks slowly toward Liam, like he or she is injured. The person is wearing an old jacket; the hood pulled up. The person is dirty, and the closer the person gets to Liam, the more he can smell whoever it is. The person smells like a sewer.

When the person reaches Liam, he or she holds onto his shoulders in order not to fall.

"Help me . . ." she says. It's Alice. She loses her strength and falls to the ground at Liam's feet.

Liam crouches down and takes a closer look at her face. "It's her, boys," he says into a microphone under his collar. "Let's go."

More than a dozen masked members of the police unit emerge from the darkness and handcuff Alice, who is now unconscious. They place her in a black van.

A few months ago, Liam drove Alice and himself to the hospital for them to get stitched up and stop the bleeding from the bullet wounds made by Emilio.

The French government questioned Liam straightaway. He explained that their relationship was strictly sexual, and she never mentioned anything about President Caron, neither did she ever shown any signs of playing a double role.

When Liam got Alice onto the TV crew for the New Year's show at the president's house, he did it through many intermediaries and successfully hid his real name, keeping it out of the story.

Liam played this one nicely.

Alice has seduced and tricked many men in her life, but now she knows what it's like to be played . . .

CHAPTER 46

When The Past Grabs You

Meanwhile at Victor's house . . .

Bogdan has almost fully recovered, but Victor is still recovering from Lucy leaving him. He sees the words from her letter every time he closes his eyes, even in his sleep. They're stuck in his head, and he's deeply depressed and hasn't done much for the past month.

Leo and D are chasing each other in the fenced yard. It's the beginning of February, but it's sunny, around 1:30 p.m. Victor and Bogdan are in the living room.

"Listen," Bogdan says. "For the past month we've barely talked. I understand that this is very heavy on you, but you can't be like this forever, man." He tries to use a mild tone, so Victor will open up a bit. "Look at Leo and D," he says, trying to cheer Victor up. "Doesn't that makes you happy? Hey man, you're free now."

Victor remains silent as he stares at the coffee table.

"I'm not saying we should have a party now," Bogdan continues. "I'm just saying let's walk outside, go for a drive, or even turn on the TV for the first time in a month to start with."

Victor still doesn't react.

"You remember what the people from the Destiny told us about the person who hired us and that letter that was read on live TV? There's the Meng Virus, the Angel Mosquitos, and all the other presidents being killed on the same night. Let's see what's happening in the world now. You and me had a deal. We're weren't to turn on our phones or the TV and completely isolate ourselves for a month in order to leave everything behind, not to think about it, and to have a fresh start. Now is the time to see what's happening out there, outside of your house." He takes the remote from the table and turns on the TV.

As Bogdan scrolls through the channels, Victor moves only his eyeballs to see what's on the TV. Bogdan becomes curious as the news on WNC says "BREAKING," and he turns up the volumes.

Natalie Archer is on the screen. She is holding a microphone as she stands in a dark alley. "She was arrested less than half an hour ago, right here on this spot. The people of France are excited because they believe she will finally face justice." As she talks, Alice's picture pops up in the top-right corner of the screen.

Victor jumps off the couch. "No fucking way!" His eyes are wide open, and he's standing there like he's just seen a ghost.

"Wait, what?" Bogdan asks, confused.

"Oh, my life is a joke, isn't it? Give me the remote please!" Victor takes the remote from Bogdan and turns the volume to maximum.

A man in an army uniform who looks like some kind of army general appears on the TV. "Alice Hill is being held in a secure location, and we have our best detectives and special forces taking care of her," he says. "The whole of

France owes a great debt of gratitude to Lieutenant Liam Mercier for organizing the effort to capture one of the biggest enemies in the country's history."

Natalie Archer takes over, describing what happened on New Year's Eve at Elysée Palace and how the president was murdered.

"Wait, what happened to you?" Bogdan is shocked that Victor is "alive" again.

Victor shakes his head while turning off the TV. "There's just no end to this; its endless."

"For fuck's sake, tell me what's happening!" Bogdan is angry now.

"The girl who you just saw on TV, the one who killed the French president at the same time we were, well, doing something similar, Alice Hill, she and I have a history." He's more than alive now; he's walking around.

"What kind of history?"

"I was in Bali having a little getaway with my friends a few years ago, before I met Lucy." He stops for a second. "I fell off my surfboard, and in that clumsy fall, the board hit me in the back of the head, and I lost consciousness. The next thing I remember I was lying on the beach, and I opened my eyes and saw, well, the most beautiful girl ever. So, I asked . . ." His eyes get teary. "I asked . . . 'Am I in heaven?'" She knew that was a compliment for her."

"And then?" Bogdan asks, intrigued.

"We spent the most amazing two weeks together. I will never forget that. Then we went back to our regular jobs and our countries, and she didn't respond to any of my messages and blocked me on her social networks, which I barely used, but it was the only way to reach her in Australia."

"Oh . . . weird," Bogdan says, frowning.

"Right? I thought so as well. I never found out why she did that. I wondered if she was married or something. Then I met Lucy. Lucy is fantastic. At the beginning of our relationship, I was still thinking about Alice, but as time passed, it faded a bit, and Lucy took over. I fell in love with Lucy. She's the love of my life. She's perfect. She's everything I ever wanted. Lucy has always had only one thing missing though: she's not Alice."

"No, don't tell me," Bogdan says, standing up. "I already know."

Victor nods with determination as he looks into his friend's eyes. "We need to save Alice!"

"Oh, shut your mouth!" Bogdan says. "How the fuck can we do that?" Despite his protests, he prefers this side of Victor to the one he has just spent a month living with.

"I have absolutely no idea!" Victor says, and they both laugh.

CHAPTER 47

A Day In Connor's Life

It's a gorgeous day in Bern, Switzerland. The sun is up, the wind is mild, and lots of people are walking the streets and taking advantage of a warm, sunny day in February.

The way the city is built around the Aare River gives it a unique look. With some mountains in the background, it looks like the most magnificent postcard.

Connor opens the door of his beautiful, rustic wooden house and inhales the fresh air. He walks toward the gate of his fenced yard, which is a mixture of snow and grass at the moment as the sun melts the winter cover and reveals a beautiful green carpet below. The same thing is happening everywhere in Switzerland. It will remain that way for the next few days until the snow covers everything again.

He walks casually and looks around. Couples, older people, kids, everyone wants to take advantage of the sunny day in February.

An older guy with a kid walking his dog passes by, and Connor stops for a moment to address the kid. "Hi, can I pet your dog?"

"Yes! His name is Boss!" The little boy is happy that someone is paying attention to his dog.

"I see," Connor replies, smiling. "He definitely looks like a Boss. What's the name of his breed?" He knows, of course, but he wants to hear it from the kid.

"He's an English bulldog!"

"Wow, and what does Boss like to do the most?"

The kid smiles. "He likes to sleep a lot!"

Connor chuckles. "Can Boss have a treat?" He pulls a few dog treats out of his pocket. He always carries some when he walks around.

"Oh yes, he loves treats!"

"Here . . ." Connor feeds them to the dog. "You guys enjoy this beautiful day." He keeps on walking.

Connor loves dogs, but he can never have one because a dog is a liability in his line of work.

After a few minutes, he reaches a small grocery store and goes inside.

"Good afternoon, Mr. Jones!" Julia, a cashier in her early twenties, has known Connor for a few years now from working in the store.

"Good afternoon, Julia! How's your day going so far?"

"Good, but honestly, I can't wait to finish my shift to go and meet my friends down by the river."

Connor smiles. "It's too early for swimming, Julia," he jokes and then starts putting some groceries into his shopping basket.

Julia laughs. "I'm crazy, but not that crazy!"

"I don't know about that . . ." Connor says, smiling.

"Let's see," Julia says when he returns to the counter a few minutes later. "Ham, eggs, mozzarella . . . I see, it's pizza day again?" She raises one eyebrow.

"You should be a detective," Connor says, giving her a quick smile.

"When am I going to try that 'Mr. Jones Pizza?'" she asks, her eyes narrowing and her lips pressing together.

"I'll save you some," Connor says. "But I promise, it's not that good."

Julia doesn't care about pizza. She likes Connor and is always trying to get him to ask her on a date, but she tries not to be too obvious.

Julia is really something, young but yet mature, beautiful but very polite, and her smile, well, once guys see it, they forget what they wanted to buy in the first place.

Connor thinks Julia was very interesting and beautiful, very young too. *But when was that the problem?*

However, Connor can never have a woman either because, like a dog, a woman is a liability.

With a woman, he would have love and family, kids. But kids are a disadvantage, a family is a disadvantage, and so is love.

CHAPTER 48

You Jinxed Us!

"There must be a way!" Victor insists, pacing around the room.

Bogdan shakes his head as he sits in a chair. "I don't see one."

"Come on, we need to be more positive."

"And more realistic!" Bogdan says, standing up. "We can't save her; there's no way. It's a fact. We were good while working for The Nobodies because of all the information they sent us. It was all there: details, movements, timing, where, why. We were just there to pull the trigger."

Victor is listening to him, but he doesn't reply.

"You know, we're not that special," Bogdan continues. "Lots of other people could have done what we did with all that information."

"But why us then, hmm? There must be a reason why we of all people were chosen and not some ex-military professionals."

"It's too risky," Bogdan says. "They're too connected. All those ex-special forces, they all know each other one way or another. Governments also have their files, from the time they worked for the government. Hiring them would create a great risk of being tracked down. The only reason why these Nobodies are capable of organizing all of this is their secrecy. How would you or me track them down? Hmm?

We know nothing about them. Even if The Nobodies decided not to pay us at the end of the mission, we couldn't have done anything about it."

Victor is slowly understanding what Bogdan is saying.

"You're a restaurant manager," Bogdan says, "and I'm a footballer, a semi-professional. Who will ever search for us as the murderers of all these presidents? We're perfect for this. We're, well, we're nobodies. It's been a month, and I would say they have nothing yet because no one has come knocking on your door." Bogdan finishes his monologue with his index finger pointed at the door.

Just then, someone knocks on that very door.

Their eyes open wide, and they're instantly covered in sweat as Leo and D stand in front of the door, guarding the territory from whoever is knocking.

"Did you order any food?" Victor whispers, looking at Bogdan and hoping he will say "yes."

Bogdan raises one eyebrow and shakes his head. "No."

"You jinxed us!" Victor hisses. "You said no one has come knocking on that door! There you go. Happy now?"

"Jinx? What? Oh, grow up!" Bogdan says, waving Victor's remarks away. "Where's the gun!" He starts looking around.

"You don't need one," a female voice says from behind the door.

They look at each other. "Shit!"

Bogdan takes a deep breath and opens the door while Victor is with the dogs, making sure they're ready to jump on the intruder, if needed.

Bogdan opens the door and sees an older lady with short white hair and small blue eyes looking at him. Before he can say anything, Vera enters the house.

Bogdan has no choice but to step aside. "Sure, come in, be our guest." He's still very confused.

The dogs come and smell her. Vera gives them each a treat, and they go to another room to eat them.

Who carries dog treats with them all the time? Victor wonders. *She must have known that we have dogs.*

"If I can have some time alone with Bogdan, I would really appreciate it," she says, looking at Victor.

Victor and Bogdan have so many questions, but they are very curious what this "old lady" has to say.

Bogdan gives Victor a nod, indicating that he will be fine. Victor goes into the same room as Leo and D to give them some privacy.

"I want to avoid any drama," Vera begins, "any emotion, anything that can slow down this conversation. First, I will speak, and you will listen. After that, you can ask a few questions, understand?" She's very straightforward.

"Sure, OK," Bogdan says, nodding.

"I know who you are," Vera begins, "and I know what you did. Well, basically, I know everything about you."

She stares directly into his eyes. Bogdan wants to say something, but he remembers that he shouldn't ask anything yet.

"I know the people who gave you the tasks, and I know that it's over now. That's why I'm here."

Bogdan nods. He's listening very carefully.

"For many, many years, I've been watching you through other people's eyes, through cameras, but I've never been able to meet you in person considering the circumstances. I don't know how much life I have left in me, but I've decided not to spend a single minute more, being a stranger to my only son."

Bogdan loses his confident posture and blinks a couple of times. *What's happening?*

"I have a lot to say," Vera continues, "and I'm sure you have a lot of questions but—"

"But you gave me to the orphanage!" he says, interrupting her.

"Yes. It was for the best, and I was right. If you'll listen further . . ." She's speaking a bit louder now.

"Wait, wait." Bogdan rubs his eyes and then looks at her again. "You're my mother?"

"I told you it's a lot to take in, but hopefully, in the end, everything will make more sense."

"How can I trust what you say?" Bogdan asks, stepping backward.

"Your dog, D, has a chip inside her neck. It has a microphone and a GPS, so I can always hear you and know your location in order to protect you," she says, trying to justify her actions.

"Protect me?" He thinks about the old guy who gave him the dog after saving him from the river. "So that guy on the boat, you sent him to help me and give me the dog?"

Vera nods. "Yes." She's hoping he's getting it now.

"Maybe you should have saved me from the broken ribs and being thrown from the bridge in the first place," Bogdan says.

She shakes her head quickly. "Too obvious."

His eyes go wide. "Too . . . obvious?"

"The other members of the organization can't know that you're my son. I don't think I need to tell you why. You can figure that one out on your own."

Bogdan rubs the bullet scars on his left leg with his left hand. "And that ship, Destiny, that wasn't destiny at all, right?" It all comes back to him.

"It was just me trying to protect you. I'm not looking for any excuses. You probably just wanted a normal life and a normal mother, and you couldn't have it, but now . . ."

"What?"

"Now you can."

Vera tells Bogdan about The Nobodies. She tells him almost everything, except about Connor. She doesn't mention his name, how he looks, or anything. She wants to stay away from his big project. She isn't part of it, and she doesn't want to get involved with it, but he's still her best friend if he needs her for anything else.

After a while, Victor, enters the room. "I don't want to interrupt your reunion, but . . ." He explains that he heard most of it from the other room.

"I need to speak with you as well," she says, looking at Victor.

"Me? Oh, I know who my mother is."

"But you don't know who your Grandpa Luigi really was . . ."

CHAPTER 49

The Best Nobody

Victor is a bit confused. He knows he's about to find out something shocking.

"You know your Grandpa Luigi was a bit shady and mysterious, but this will clarify things," Vera says. "Thirty years ago, we were still building The Nobodies, and we looked all over the world for the right candidates. Luigi, your grandfather, was in his early forties, not so much a 'grandpa' at that time. I came to Florence with a team of six people, planning to lure Luigi into a hotel room and then explain our offer. We had orders to kill him if he refused. Luigi was the profile we needed: smart, confident, strong, and with a clean record, even though he had a charge or two in his youth, he was never convicted. Our leader really wanted Luigi to become a member of The Nobodies."

Victor and Bogdan sit down, focused on the story.

"So, I was sitting in a street bar in front of the Cattedrale di Santa Maria del Fiore, in Florence, just a few tables from the table where Luigi was sitting and reading the newspaper while enjoying a glass of white wine. It was midday, very nice weather." She stops for a moment and smiles. "Anyway," she turns serious again quickly. "The idea was to send a beautiful girl to a table next to him to catch his attention and lure him to a hotel room, where my team and I would take over.

"We knew that Luigi had been married to his high school sweetheart, Olivia, since they were eighteen years old, and they had a child, Elena, your mother. But we also knew that although Luigi loved Olivia and had spent his entire life with her, from time to time he liked to have some adventures with younger girls, which Olivia obviously wasn't aware of.

"We hired the most beautiful Italian brunette, named Donatella, and she came in a short red dress. It was impossible not to notice her. Not just for Luigi but for everyone.

"As I mentioned before, I was just a few tables away from their tables, so I could observe the situation and guide my team through the small microphone that I had hidden in my earring. I saw Luigi notice Donatella, scan her from head to toe, and then continue reading the paper.

"The weird part was, he was looking in my direction and not Donatella's, so I was wondering if he suspected something. Suddenly, Luigi stood up and started walking straight toward my table. He pulled out a chair and sat down with me. I told my team to be ready for action, that we might have been discovered.

"The first thing he said to me was . . ." She stops for a moment and takes a deep breath. "He told me, 'If you were a city, you would be more beautiful than Florence.'" She struggles to continue. Cold-blooded Vera is overflowing with memories.

"Well, and I, I opened my mouth, but not a single word came out. I was speechless. That was many years ago, and your grandpa looked like Robert De Niro in his best days.

Black hair, white shirt, black leather jacket, and that charming smile.

I was thirty-five, not that young, certainly not like Donatella, so I was confused but flattered that someone like him could walk past Donatella and make advances at me.

"The funny part is, my team was asking me how to proceed, and I still couldn't say a word. Luigi and I, eventually we got into a conversation, and when I left to go to the bathroom, I let my team know that we were aborting the mission and would continue the following day."

Bogdan and Victor are confused but focused. They're listening to the story like kids listen to beautiful fairytales before they go to sleep. Victor is a bit sad that Grandpa Luigi isn't that "perfect" anymore and that he wasn't entirely faithful to Grandma Olivia, but hearing the story about his youthful days is amusing.

"To make a long story short," Vera continues, "we became close, and I tried not to get him hired as a Nobody, but my leader would have me killed if I refused, so I explained what it was about, and Luigi was actually pretty excited. He would make a great amount of money, and he would kill only bad people. He thought it was a fair deal. The only bad thing was, we couldn't see each other anymore. Our relationship needed to end. I was his boss, along with three other people, as I mentioned to you before. Of course, we found ways to see each other from time to time, but it wasn't enough, and we were risking our lives each time. He worked for us for many years. Our leader was right; Luigi was our best hire ever until . . . until he decided to go against the committee.

He wanted out, and he wanted me to come with him. I said no, I couldn't, and he knew that.

"Then suddenly, your Grandma Olivia passed away, and Luigi was so sure that our leader had something to do with it. Even though it wasn't true, which I guaranteed him, he would not stop. He continued trying to expose the committee.

"This might be hard for you to hear, but he didn't just die. He was poisoned by his younger partner, whom he trusted blindly, even with his life, which cost him exactly that in the end."

Victor is angry, but he doesn't say anything because he wants to hear the entire story first.

"But before Luigi was poisoned, and to give you one more reason why he was poisoned, he managed to steal some very valuable information from our leader and hide it somewhere. It hasn't been found even today. That was the moment when our leader decided that The Nobodies would not be allowed to meet us, the leaders, anymore. He couldn't risk being betrayed again.

"We searched his entire house, including the garage—we knew about his secret hole and the fact that you used it from time to time—but we never found the files."

"You keep saying 'our leader,'" Bogdan says. "We can't know his name?"

Vera shakes her head. "No, it's for your own safety. All I'm saying is I'm doing this because it's over for the three of us. The rest of the leaders and I observed you a lot, and we knew it wasn't in your interest to do any harm to the committee. However, even what I just told you will get you killed if you try to share it, but I know you're smarter than that, and you'll gain nothing by doing so."

"So, the leader is the one who hired all of us for these presidential assassinations?" Bogdan asks. "The Meng Virus? The mosquitos? All him?"

"Yes. It's his own project. Two of the other leaders are dead. I'm not involved or in his way, so it's only him organizing all of that."

"May I at least know the name of the person, my Grandpa Luigi's 'young partner,' who betrayed him and killed him?"

"Yes, but know that if you try anything, you'll get yourself killed. His name is Emilio."

"Wait," Bogdan says. "If you were in love with Luigi, when did you met my father?"

Vera looks at him and takes a deep breath. "Remember, I said this was thirty years ago . . ." She's hoping he'll catch the hint.

"No way!" Victor yells.

"Luigi . . . He was my father, wasn't he?" Like a hammer hitting a nail, this revelation knocks him back onto the sofa.

"Yes, he was," Vera says calmly.

CHAPTER 50

Natalie Archer vs. The Secretary Of Defense

Connor always watches the 8:00 p.m. news on WNC and follows the progress of the Angel Mosquitos and the Meng Virus around the world.

He's sitting in his home, and it's snowing again outside, so he makes himself some hot chocolate and then settles in to watch TV.

It has been already more than a month, but the main topic is still the events that occurred on New Year's Eve, the Angel Mosquitos, and the Meng Virus. Natalie Archer is having a conversation with USA Secretary of Defense, Jake Collins.

"How is it possible that someone could organize and execute such horrific events in multiple countries against the most protected people in the world, and over a month later, only Alice Hill has been arrested, accused of murdering the French president? Where are the rest of the killers? And who has the power to organize all of these things so perfectly, shaking up the entire world in just one night?"

"Well, through the centuries, the element of surprise has been shown as the most effective military technique," Secretary Collins says. "Which obviously this, let's call him or her Person X, seeing as we don't know if it's a male or female, is clearly familiar with."

"But aren't security forces trained for such things?" Natalie asks. "The only way that someone would dare to attack a world leader would be the element of surprise, so in the end, it should not be a surprise at all. Correct?" She loves to place her important guests in difficult situations.

"Well, yes," Collins admits. "However, without giving excuses, to do such a thing on New Year's Eve, that was really low."

"Yet brilliant," Natalie points out.

"I mean . . ." Collins is lost, unable to continue.

"Is it be correct that this Person X actually prevented nuclear war and did the world a favor? Considering the letter that Person X sent, that's pretty strong proof, don't you agree? As secretary of defense, you know what impact a nuclear war would have on this planet, I'm sure." She smiles.

"No, absolutely not," Collins says, shaking his head. "That's all nonsense."

"We have confirmed fifty-two thousand deaths around the globe by the so-called Angel Mosquitos. A few weeks ago it was only a little over two thousand, and so far the Meng Virus has killed over one hundred thousand people in China and India. Is the government considering the idea of disarming its nuclear weapons? If not, how many deaths will it take to convince you to do so?"

Natalie continues ripping Collins apart for the next twenty-five minutes, making Connor chuckle a couple of times. He could swear she's on his side.

To be fair, a good amount of the population actually trusts Connor's letter. No one knows for sure, but some people believe it's all true. Many others believe he's the worst terrorist in the world and needs to be brought to justice.

CHAPTER 51

The "Hero" Of France

It's dark except for one light that's coming through a 10 cm-wide window that looks out onto an inner courtyard. The window is in a concrete wall. It doesn't have any glass in it. It's just 30 cm long and 10 cm wide, so whoever is inside the room can see through it and get some fresh air, but it isn't that friendly now during winter when the cold air sneaks under the skin.

Alice's cell is made almost completely out of concrete— bed, walls, window, desk, stool. Only the toilet and sink/ water fountain and the metal doors behind the metal bars are not made of concrete.

The French government has put Alice in their most secure supermax prison, called Le Beton, which translates as "The Concrete" in English.

Alice is sitting on her bed, thinking about her life, past, present, and, well, she doesn't seem to have much of a future. She cried all of her tears in previous days, and now she's just empty.

The prison staff has given her the minimum of every-thing compared to other prisoners, but they don't beat her or torture her. They don't want to affect her upcoming trial. They all want the highest sentence to be announced.

She's skinny, and she feels cold. Her spirit is broken.

The last person she trusted was Liam, and he betrayed her. Alice remembers David and how he tried to kill her, and now she's wondering if anyone has ever made worse choices in men than her.

The metal door opens, and light brightens the cell. She sees the shadow of a man. The door closes, and the man stands between the metal bars and the metal doors, which have over a meter between them.

As her eyes get used to the dark again, she recognizes the person standing in front of her: Liam.

"The hero of France," Alice says sarcastically. Of course, Liam's plan is clear.

"I'm glad you understand," he says with a proud, cynical expression.

Alice knows that Liam let her do this, so he could catch her and become famous and respected.

"How do you live with yourself?" she asks. "You killed the president as much as I did. You knew about it before it happened, and you let it happen, so you could do what you have done and become a fake hero. You even helped me become part of the TV crew. I guess you hid that information as well. You're a bigger murderer than I am. You're a . . . you're disgusting." Her eyes narrow in hate.

"It was clever, don't you think?" He can't remove the smirk from his face.

"Just fucking leave," Alice says. She's empty, dead inside.

"Don't you feel lonely here?" Liam asks. "I came to keep you company, baby." He's pushing her to react, but she's better than that. She just ignores him.

"I'm just here to tell you that by the end of the week, you'll know your future. I mean, it doesn't make any difference to you, does it? Being sentenced to one or ten life sentences? The fact is, you'll never poison anyone again. You murderer." He turns to leave.

"Don't be so sure," she replies, a smirk on her face. "Remember, I killed your president, and you're a way easier mission than that." She turns around and looks out the window, knowing that isn't going to happen, but she needed to say something to feel better.

"You're pathetic, Alice," Liam says. "Have a good sleep, and keep dreaming on your concrete bed. I'm going home to have some wine and relax in my jacuzzi with some music. After all, I'm the hero of France." The metal door opens, and Liam leaves her cell.

CHAPTER 52

Just One Minute, Please!

It takes some discussion, but eventually, everyone is on the same page. It's shocking news for both men. Victor's Grandpa Luigi was Vera's lover, Bogdan's father, and one of the best Nobodies ever. Not to mention the only one who ever dared to go against Connor.

"You mentioned that the leader knows you're here and sharing all of this with us, right?" Bogdan asks.

"As I mentioned, you guys aren't considered threats, and as long is that's the case, you'll live. Everything I told you is purely for you to know more about yourselves, because we already know more about you than you do."

"So, how many people like Victor and I are left?" Bogdan asks.

"A few," Vera replies. "Either they earned their freedom like you, or they're dead. There is no middle. The Nobodies project is closed for good." She wants to put an end to the discussion.

Victor looks at Bogdan, who knows exactly what Victor is about to ask.

"But not all of them are dead or free," Victor says.

Vera looks at him, confused.

"Alice Hill . . . she's neither dead nor free, correct?" he almost whispers.

"That will be handled very soon," Vera says. "As I mentioned, there is no middle ground."

"Handled?" Bogdan asks. "You mean someone will kill her in prison?"

Vera nods.

"You need to stop them!" Victor says, raising his voice and stepping closer to her.

"Excuse me?" Vera says, sinking back into the sofa.

"She and I have a bit of history."

"Wait, we don't know anything about this," Vera says. "Are you two related?"

"She saved his life," Bogdan says. "When they were younger, they dated for a short time, but it's never faded from Victor's mind."

"Oh," Vera says, then shakes her head. "I'm sorry, but nothing can be done."

"What do you mean?" Victor asks. "Can't you just call off your killer?"

"It's not *my* killer. I'm out of the committee, remember? But I know the leader's opinion about this. Someone will get rid of her." She looks into the distance, avoiding eye contact with both of them.

"Bastard," Victor says. "She just followed his orders, and now he's going to cut the loose ends? What kind of leader is that?" He turns his back to her.

"Hey, what do you think it takes?" Vera asks. She's upset for a moment, but she calms down quickly. "A man like him, for over thirty years, a complete ghost in this world. What do you think it takes? Yes, it takes some very hard decisions and cruel things, but he and we saved millions of lives!" She does not like being judged.

"But what if she's like us?" Bogdan asks, "harmless to the committee and not planning to say anything about The Nobodies? Maybe she just wants to be free and doesn't give a damn about what happened in the past." He stands up, pacing.

"It doesn't work that way," Vera says. "We don't operate by hoping for things, like hoping she won't talk."

"So if Bogdan was in her place, you would do the same thing?" Victor asks, "because that's the way you operate?" He looks her straight in the eye.

"It's not the same," Vera says, breathing a bit faster.

Victor sits on the sofa to think.

"I should be going," Vera says, standing up. "I'll be staying in Canada for a few days if you want to spend some time together. Here's my phone number. I'd be happy to see you." She gives a clumsy hug to Bogdan and then heads for the door.

"Wait," Victor says. Vera turns around. "I only need one favor," he says. "Can you do it for me, please?"

Vera looks at him, a bit angry about the things he said earlier.

"Could you ask the leader to call me?" he asks. Vera shakes her head, but Victor continues. "He knows how to hide the call, to hide his location, his voice, everything. I just need one minute of his time. Tonight, right now, please?" He looks at her with pleading eyes.

"Even if he calls you, he'll give you the same answer I gave you," she says as she continues to leave.

"But it would still be a big favor for me. I need to at least try."

She looks at him for a moment. He reminds her of Luigi. Finally, she sighs. "Sure. Let's close this book once and for all." She knows it's better to do this than to risk him trying something on his own and getting himself and Bogdan killed or exposing the group.

I'll do it for Luigi, she thinks.

CHAPTER 53

A Lonely Night

Alice is looking through the small window in her cell, moments after Liam left. It's all so unreal for her. It was her choice to become a Nobody, but she couldn't have lived with herself knowing she could have done something to save her dad, but she chose not to.

Did Dad see the news and how his "baby girl" is actually a killer? she wonders. *What's he thinking now?*

This is my destiny. Everything has led to this moment. How did I think this was going to end? Liam is a piece of shit, but he's right; I'm a murderer. They only know about their president, but there are many others. This is my destiny. This is my end.

Alice tries to think about happy times, some good parts of her life, and it's all before she started killing people for The Nobodies. She remembers Victor again. She wonders if she hadn't been too scared to let herself into that romance, would her life have been any different? Alice didn't answer any of his messages because she wasn't ready for a relationship, at least that was her thinking at the time. *Did I make good choices in my life?*

Time, memories, and herself, that's all that's left for Alice in that dark concrete cell.

Alice tries to suppress thoughts of the future and how the rest of her days will be like this cold, lonely night.

CHAPTER 54

The Hook

At the end of the conversation, Vera leaves the house for a moment to call Connor and see if it's possible to give Victor a call and get this over with.

"Hey, I'll be right back!" Victor says to Bogdan as he runs up the stairs.

"Wait, where . . ." But Victor is already in his bedroom on the upper floor.

Fifteen minutes passes before Victor returns.

"Is everything OK?" Bogdan asks.

"It will be," Victor says, winking at Bogdan before Vera enters the house again.

"OK, he's going to call," she says.

"Yes! Thank you!" Victor holds his left fist high.

"You need to speak to him in front of me, so we can be sure you don't record him or do anything else suspicious. Got it?"

Victor shrugs. "Anything you guys want."

Vera notices that Victor is a bit different, more confident.

A moment later, Victor's phone rings, and he places it on the table in front of them, then puts it on speakerphone.

"One minute," Connor says. "Go."

Victor takes a deep breath. "OK. Thank you for calling. I really appreciate—"

"Fifty seconds." Connor isn't interested in gratitude.

"I don't know if Vera mentioned anything, but I would like to ask you to call off the person who you hired to kill Alice in prison."

"No. Forty seconds."

"And not just that. I would like you to help me save her from that prison." As if he didn't hear Connor's refusal, Victor continues with his request.

"Nonsense. No. Thirty seconds." It confuses Connor for a bit that Victor is even daring to request something.

"I don't need much," Victor continues. "I only need you to create a mission in The Nobodies app with the details of the prison and how to save Alice and two to three ex-Nobodies to help." He continues in the same rhythm like he hasn't heard Connor say "no" multiple times.

"The Nobodies project is done, as you are aware," Connor says. "I will not go against my word and contact the people to whom I promised freedom. It's done. No more. Ten seconds left."

"Make it optional if someone wants extra cash," Victor says. "I'll pay for it from the money I made during my time. I'm really not asking much!"

"It's too risky," Connor says, "and unnecessary and not what we do in the first place. Goodbye."

"Connor!" Victor screams into the phone.

Vera looks at Victor in shock. How does he know his name?

The room is silent for nearly half a minute.

"Vera, are you there?" Connor asks. "What's going on?"

"He didn't hear it from me; I swear," she says, her voice shaking. "I don't know how he knows!"

Bogdan looks at Victor, unsure if he should be happy or terrified by this development.

"Maybe I can clarify things," Victor says. He's the only person who isn't freaking out.

"You have my attention," Connor says. He's still too powerful to be scared by this. However, he will not have peace of mind if he just hangs up.

"I have the file," Victor says. "My Grandpa Luigi's file. About you and everyone else."

Vera closes her eyes and exhales.

"And you would like to use that to blackmail me to help you save Alice Hill?"

"No, I like to think I'm smarter than that. I'm aware of what you can do, and I don't want to play any games with you."

"So you'll just hand over the file to Vera, problem solved?" Connor knows that isn't going to happen.

"Not exactly. You see, I don't think you're a cold-blooded killer. I'm starting to understand what you want and the way you do things, and I don't think you'd kill someone just because."

"It might surprise you," Connor says, his voice flat.

"Here's what I suggest," Victor continues. "I want Alice out of prison, a few fake passports, and a new life for her, which is a piece of cake for you, and you want this file, which, to be honest, means nothing to me. It's just trouble, and I'll be happy to hand it over to you." The deal seems fair to Victor.

"It still sounds like blackmail to me," Connor replies.

"Not exactly," Victor says. "You see, you're not exposing yourselves at all. You send an optional mission on the app. That way, if someone chooses to participate, it's not by force. They have a simple choice. The other thing is, for you to get info about the prison and the best way to save Alice is an easy thing. For me, it's nearly impossible. Easy, right?" Victor hopes if he stays positive, stops begging, and keeps pushing, he might get what he wants.

"I can have my people in your house in less than five minutes," Connor says. "That's even easier."

"I'm sure you can, but I repeat, I'm not a threat."

"You sure sound like one."

"I gain nothing by exposing you. However, on the other hand, I must say, because of The Nobodies, my wife left me, my dog almost died, my grandpa got killed, and my life was almost ruined. If I don't save Alice, well, being alive or dead, doesn't make a lot of difference to me. And let's face it, nobody in the world apart from me knows in which bloody desert or mountain that file is. Not even you with all your power can find it, believe me, but once you have it in your hands after so many years, at least you'll be able to sleep peacefully knowing that nobody in this world can blackmail you for anything."

"I'll think about it," Connor says. He needs to have that file in his hands. His people have been searching for it for years.

Victor wants to explode with happiness, but he keeps his cool.

"This is what needs to happen in the meantime," Connor says. "Vera will stay there with you, and at no point will you be out of her sight."

Vera wants to say something, but the plan is fine with her. She'll get to spend more time with Bogdan, and it's actually better if she's there, so she can control the situation.

"Thank you Con—" Before Victor can finish, Connor hangs up.

"Very dangerous," Vera says, shaking her head. "What you did. We better keep one eye open tonight."

They all look at each other, knowing the truth of her words.

CHAPTER 55

The World Now

The majority of the population is in a mild panic. If the deaths from the Meng Virus and the Angel Mosquitos are happening near them and their country or city, people tend to panic way more.

In Denmark, there is the smallest number of cases. Drug usage is low, cigarettes are not very popular, and the number of people with serious transmittable illnesses is low, so people seem to be living a normal life.

On the other hand, there have been 150,000 deaths between China and India, which are the primary targets of the Meng Virus. Add to that 22,000 deaths from the Angel Mosquitos just in China, and the level of panic all over the country is high.

In India and China, a state of emergency is announced, and people are forbidden to leave their homes except once a month to buy food and other essentials. When they do go out, they need to stay three meters away from everyone else.

This has been the situation for less than two months, and people are already tired and upset, continuously asking the government to disarm the nuclear weapons, so life can return to normal, but the governments still disagree.

The governments of China and India have promised their people that their best doctors and scientists are working on developing a vaccine and that so far, that's the best way to end the Meng Virus.

The Angel Mosquitos however, are still multiplying, and it's only going to get worse. The entire world has become aware and are taking them more seriously as time passes.

As Connor planned and as Tao Woo made possible, their victims are only smokers, drug users, alcoholics, and people with deadly transmittable diseases, such as AIDS, tuberculosis, pneumonia, malaria, Zika, and others. Doctors around the world are aware of this and are advising sick people to stay at home and close all windows and for smokers and drug users not to use such things. Despite these precautions, Angel Mosquitos are still finding their way into people's homes just like any regular mosquito before them, so the actual solution for seriously sick people is almost nonexistent.

The new leaders of the countries affected by the New Year's Eve assassinations—North Korea, China, Pakistan, India, Israel, and especially the USA—are still searching furiously for Person X, who coordinated all of it and the killers who executed the plan.

The UK and Russia's governments are not involved in any of that. They don't announce it publicly, but they are aware that Person X actually did them a favor by eliminating traitors in their midst.

And yet, the governments are not planning to disarm their billions of dollars' worth of nuclear equipment anytime soon.

All of these countries, except the UK and Russia, are strongly pressuring the French government to find out more from Alice in order to help find information on all the other assassins, and they are requesting the death penalty for her, though the death penalty hasn't been an option in France since 1981. The highest punishment is a life sentence.

Alice's trial will be broadcast live on all major TV stations starting the morning of February 22, 2020.

It's expected to break all records for the number of viewers following the trial on TV or online.

Victor is still expecting an answer from Connor, to see if he will accept his proposition or if he will send someone to find the SD card and kill Alice in prison before the trial even starts.

CHAPTER 56

Better Kill Me Now

The sound of the metal door opening followed by the sound of the metal bars opening wakes Alice from the two hours of sleep that she managed to get last night on her concrete bed.

Three prison guards cuff her arms and legs and walk her down the hallway. As she walks, a big, tattooed female prisoner approaches them, guarded only by a small female guard.

This is it, Alice thinks. *The one who kills me in the hallway for The Nobodies, so I don't stand trial.*

The big woman looks at Alice with hate in her eyes and continues walking in her direction.

Cold, hungry, and scared to the bone, Alice starts shaking, and the moment they pass close to each other, expecting to be stabbed or shot, Alice closes her eyes and stops breathing, turning her head slightly in the opposite direction.

A moment later, she feels a strong push from behind.

"Keep walking," the fat male guard behind Alice says. "Nobody told you to stop."

Alice opens her eyes and realizes the big woman has already passed her, and nothing happened. She exhales and continues walking.

The guards take Alice to the shower area, remove her clothes, and spray her with ice-cold water from a hose that presses Alice to the wall so hard and so suddenly that she almost smacks her head against it.

To the surprise of many, especially Alice, she arrives in the courtroom alive.

"Members of the jury," the judge says, "your duty today will be to determine whether the defendant is guilty or not guilty based only on the facts and evidence provided in this case. The prosecution has the burden of proving the defendant's guilt beyond a reasonable doubt. This burden remains on the prosecution throughout the trial. The prosecution must prove that a crime has been committed and that the defendant is the person who committed the crime. However, if you're not satisfied of the defendant's guilt to that extent, then reasonable doubt exists, and the defendant must be found not guilty."

The trial finishes much quicker than anybody expected. Alice doesn't ask for a lawyer and refuses to have one because she's sure The Nobodies will send their "lawyer" to eliminate her. She feels much safer, knowing that no one will enter her cell.

So, Alice pleads guilty and has nothing else to say. The judge prepares to announce her sentence after the jury makes its decision.

"We the jury, in the case of France against Alice Hill, have made our decision. Considering that the defendant has admitted to murdering President Thierry Caron, and considering the connection of this horrific act with the assassination of other world leaders, we request the death penalty for Alice Hill."

The people in the court start cheering, but the judge silences them, so the jury foreman can continue. "We consider a life sentence not being enough in this particular case and that the death penalty would set an example for the future, so an act like this never happens again."

Alice feels dizzy, her legs get weak, and she feels like something is pressing on her chest. She vomits on the desk in front of her.

She doesn't hear much after the judge sentences her to death.

An unexpected decision, somewhat illegal, yet, with the world currently in chaos without any solution upcoming, backed with some of the most influential governments, the jury and the judge made, or was paid to make, this decision, which is above everything, the message for Connor.

Everything is buzzing in her ears while the people around her cheer in support of the jury's decision.

"When . . . when will I . . . how . . .?" she mumbles, barely conscious, while one of the guards holds her up, so she doesn't fall over. She's trying to ask when and how she will be executed.

Alice isn't aware if it's a guard, the judge, or the jury foreman who repeats it to her, but she hears those two sentences very clearly.

"In ten days. By lethal injection."

CHAPTER 57

Is It Over?

"The death sentence." Victor stares at the TV, thinking how if he's ever caught, the punishment will probably be the same.

Victor can't imagine how Alice must be feeling, but as the camera zooms in on her face during the sentencing announcement, he sees that she's slowly losing her mind and giving up on life. What else she can do?

"On the brighter side . . .," Vera says.

Victor and Bogdan both look at her, curious what the "brighter side" of all this could be.

"The execution will happen in ten days," she says. "It's enough time to save her—if Connor decides to help." She feels a bit weird. Victor reminds her of Luigi—his movements, the way he talks. After all, Luigi was his grandfather, his mentor, and his hero.

However, even stranger is that Alice reminds Vera of a younger version of herself. Before she became old and gray, she was also a beautiful blonde with blue eyes. The only difference is the size of their eyes. Vera has small eyes, and Alice has big ones.

To Vera, it seems like she's observing her own story of struggling love and survival. She knows how it feels.

"Why hasn't he called yet?" Victor asks, visibly concerned.

"Hey, we'll save her, OK?" Bogdan says, giving Victor's shoulder a reassuring shake.

It's silent after that. Everyone just sits and thinks.

Finally, Victor's cellphone rings. He tries to answer, but he drops it on the floor.

He exhales and calms down for a second before he picks it up and answers. "Hello?"

He hears four words: "I have a plan."

CHAPTER 58

Meet Douglas Routley

The guard who is dragging Alice down the hallway has no intention of taking her back to her cell. He has been instructed differently.

Alice notices that the route is longer than usual, and despite the incredible stress she's under, thinking things can't possibly get any worse, she's concerned. Where are they taking her? Are they just going to kill her now instead of waiting for ten days?

The guard takes Alice to a dim room in the basement, then closes the door and handcuffs her to a metal chair.

A man with long gray hair and a long gray beard approaches her. "Hi, sweetheart. I'm Douglas Routley. I realize that name doesn't mean much to you now, but I promise that as long as you're alive, you won't forget it."

Douglas Routley is the kind of guy who every government has in stock to forcefully extract all necessary information from whoever it's needed. In this case, the US government isn't happy that they still don't have anything on the person who killed their president, and they know the only person who might have any information is Alice Hill.

Alice looks around and notices that the guard has left the room, leaving her alone with this creepy person.

"We don't have much time," Routley says, "but since we're going to be friends for a while, let me explain this to you. We couldn't touch you before the trial because it was going out live, and people around the world would have noticed if you had been abused here in prison. It would have affected the trial because everyone has human rights, blah, blah, blah. However, now it's time for the fun part. Now we can cut you into pieces, and no one will care. The world got their justice, and you'll not be seen in public anymore before you get the sweet relief of lethal injection."

"You're a psycho," Alice says, shaking her head in disbelief.

"That's correct," he replies, "but I haven't even started, sweetheart. I have ten days to pull out all, and I mean *all,* information about who else was involved and who planned all of this. The US government is paying me a large amount of money to do this. I'm so lucky to have this dream job." As he speaks, he puts on a pair of black leather gloves.

Alice doesn't have anything to hide or anyone to protect. She knows she has no more than ten days left, and she doesn't want to spend them in tremendous pain. She has watched enough movies to know what's coming from this lunatic.

"They're going to kill me in ten days. Do you really think I would hide anything?" She's in shock after the sentence, but she knows she needs to try to reason with this person.

"Oh, don't ruin the fun!" Routley says. "Surely you have some relatives who you don't want to get hurt if you don't tell the truth?"

"I was alone in this, No brothers, sisters, or kids. As a matter of fact, I killed my husband."

He pulls out a chair and sits in front of her. "How'd you do that?" he asks, smiling.

"Poison," she whispers.

"Poison? Nah, way too easy. Not a fan."

It's a very awkward situation for Alice. She knows he's going to hurt her, but she has a feeling inside her, like there's no more future for her, nothing, not even the present. Her life is ending no matter what. She's not scared though; she's just . . . empty.

"OK, let's go to more important topics. Who do you work for?" He crouches in front of her.

She explains the entire story of how she became a Nobody because of her father, how they communicate through the game app, how they pay in cash, how she killed President Caron, and anything else she thinks he wants to know. She's like an open book.

"Hmm," he says, shaking his head. "I don't know. This is too easy . . ."

"But that's—"

His loud laugh interrupts her. He laughs and laughs for over a minute.

"Hey, listen, thank you for this," he says when he finally stops. "Throughout my career, I have met people begging for their lives, saying all kinds of crap, vomiting on me, crying, but your story, I've never heard any bigger bullshit than that!" He wipes his teary eyes with a small white towel.

Alice is confused. She has never been more honest in her entire life.

"Listen," Routley says, "you're, um, quite popular on Instagram. You travel, you had a husband, a normal life, and all this is a very good cover, so whoever you work for, it's pretty good but not worth all the pain you'll feel if you don't start telling me the truth."

This feeling for Alice is even worse than a death sentence. She has given him everything he wants, but he took it as a joke, a fake story. Even scarier is she has nothing left to say, and she knows if she doesn't talk, he'll act.

"I can tell you where I buried my husband's body to confirm the story."

Routley thinks for a moment and then shrugs. "Fine. I believe you might have killed your husband. Big deal. You're a murderer; I'm aware of that, but who knows the real reason? Maybe he didn't like the dinner you prepared, and you snapped. But the other things, I mean, come on, I don't have time for this."

He stands up and hits her as hard as he can in the nose. The pain is strong, and Alice hears buzzing in her ears and feels blood pouring over her lips. Her eyes are teary, and it's difficult to breathe through her nose.

"Let me tell you something." He comes closer to her face. "The pain you just felt is just a tickle compared to what's coming if you don't start talking!"

Alice is desperate, terrified that she can't do a single thing to stop this maniac from causing her more pain. Earlier, she was terrified to find out that she only has ten more days to live. Now those ten days look like an eternity.

CHAPTER 59

Another Day In Paradise

Ice-cold water splashes on Alice's face from a wooden bucket, waking her up.

"Wake up, little angel," Routley taunts, "or should I say, 'little devil'?" He's almost singing, the tone of his voice soft.

Alice opens the eyes and tries to remember what happened last. She has no idea how long she has been in that room, tied to that chair, used as a punching bag. And worse . . .

It has been four days since she was brought to the room, and she hasn't left. The fifth night of torture is about to start. They give her just enough food and water to keep her conscious, but she refuses it and spits it out. She wants to die; it would be a relief.

Routley leaves every night with a huge black wheeled case and sleeps in a nearby motel, then returns in the morning. When the prison warden asks him why he drags the big case all the time when he could just leave it in the basement, he says that even more than torturing people, he loves sharpening his knives and other tools every night before he goes to sleep. It makes him calm and happy.

Douglas Routley is a freak.

"Listen," he says, "I've got good news—for me, not for you. I've been approved to start using my tools, since it has been four days, and it seems like you're getting immune to punches and cuts."

Alice tries to say something when she feels an unbearable pain at the back of her head. Her jaw is broken from all the punches. She can barely swallow her own saliva, and most of it drips out of her mouth.

On her arms are cuts, and a mixture of wet and dry blood is on her face. Alice is wondering how she looks, but she doesn't want to see. Her entire body is numb, and she has a fever.

"Listen, sweetheart," Routley says, "I don't think you're going to last all ten days with me, so let's get this over with now." He goes to the table and picks up something that looks like a cigar cutter.

He crouches next to her legs and places the small toe of her right foot inside the cutter. "Who's your boss?" he asks. "Who are you working for? Five seconds!"

"Don't," Alice pleads. "I told you . . . I told you so many times . . . I don't know who hired me!" She screams with her last ounce of strength before Routley chops off her small toe, and Alice passes out from the pain.

He picks up her toe and approaches a prison guard, who is always with them in the room while Routley tortures her, just in case. "Look at this little beauty!" Routley says, holding it in front of the guard's face.

The guard places a hand over his mouth as if he's ready to vomit, then waves his other hand and leaves the room.

Routley picks up his phone and calls someone the moment the guard leaves. "Boss, she doesn't know anything. She knows a bit about the app but nothing about who hired her. She has no clue. I even cut off her toe. I mean, anyone would talk five days away from lethal injection. If she doesn't talk now, she never will." He pauses, hearing only breathing on the other end. "Should I proceed with the second part of the plan?"

"Do it," Connor says.

CHAPTER 60

"And The Oscar Goes To . . ."

Routley locks the door from the inside while the guard is in the bathroom, vomiting. He opens his big black case and pulls out the body of a dead blond woman. He drags the body closer to Alice, whose face is unrecognizable from all the punches, and drops it on the floor for a moment, face up.

Routley compares the two women. They look similar enough, so he takes some blood from Alice's body and starts spreading it over the dead woman's face and arms.

The body is wearing a prisoners' uniform. Only the arms, face, and feet are bare. He has some extra blood in a plastic bottle, and he adds it to the body parts and uniform to match it with Alice's blood marks and then quickly pulls out the cigar cutter and cuts the small toe off the dead woman's right root, identical to Alice, and sprays it with some blood from the bottle.

He takes a picture of Alice tied to the chair the night before and spends the night creating the same things and adding some makeup to the face and body of the dead woman, so she looks like Alice, who is already hard to recognize with all the blood and swelling on her face.

Then Routley swaps the two of them, putting the dead woman in the chair and placing Alice in his big black case, which has only a few tools inside to create the sound of metal hitting metal while he pulls it, so nobody suspects anything.

Routley is aware of the guard's smoking habits from the days before, and he assumes that after he finishes vomiting, he will go for a cigarette. But still, he locked the door earlier with the slide bolt lock from inside just in case. He unlocks the door. Then he places his bloody clothes in the same big black case. He's ready to leave.

Someone opens the door. The guard is back.

"I'm going," Routley says. "She's passed out, and I have no use for her until she wakes up, which will probably be in three to four hours."

The guard steps toward the chair where "Alice" is tied and notices the missing toe on her right foot. No matter how many times he sees it, it will always be disgusting for him.

"Let's go," Routley says while dimming the lights like every night before. "She needs to rest, to recover a bit of energy. I still need more information from her. Make sure nobody wakes her up for at least four hours."

"Sure thing, Mr. Routley," the guard says, obviously afraid of him after all he's witnessed.

The guard locks the room, and Routley leaves like every night before, pulling his big black wheeled case behind him.

CHAPTER 61

The Exchange

A mild breeze goes through Victor's hair as *Destiny* sails on the blue, wide North Atlantic Ocean.

"Thank you for doing this with me," he says to Bogdan, who is outside near the rail at the bow.

"You're welcome," Bogdan says. "I'm curious what kind of plan Connor has for us. It still sounds impossible for only two people to get into the supermax prison and get Alice out. Not to be negative, but you understand."

Victor nods. "I understand. But the guy's a genius. That's why I believe with his plan, we can do it."

Six days earlier, just after the live TV announcement of Alice's death sentence, Connor called Victor to say he had a plan. He explained that in six days, they needed to be at certain coordinates in the middle of the North Atlantic Ocean, and then he would inform them of the next step. He also said they were to bring Luigi's SD card with him. Victor was fully aware that it might be a setup in the middle of nowhere, but had no options, and time wasn't his friend because Alice only had ten more days to live. They are there now, waiting for the next step. It's Vera's yacht, so she's there with them—also because Connor requested it.

A red-and-white helicopter appears in the distance. It looks like a medevac helicopter, complete with big red crosses on its sides. As it gets closer, it prepares to land on the yacht.

Once the helicopter lands, its side door opens. Vera, Victor, and Bogdan wait and watch to see who will come out. Vera has known Connor for many years, but Victor and Bogdan have never seen him in person.

It's intense.

A person wearing black pants, a black long-sleeved shirt, black gloves, and a black ski mask comes out of the helicopter holding a gun to Alice's head. She's conscious now but has no idea what's happening or where she is.

"The SD card, please," the masked man says.

Victor is shocked to see that Alice is already there. He doesn't know what to think. Throughout the trip, he's been mentally preparing himself to break into that prison and save her, but now she's right in front of him.

Victor runs to his cabin and grabs the SD card. As he walks slowly toward the masked person, he looks at Vera, who nods. Then he hands over the card.

The man pushes Alice toward Victor. "We gave her some basic medical assistance, but she needs more. Food and water also. ASAP." He climbs back into the helicopter, and it lifts off the yacht, flying away to an unknown location.

Alice is in bad shape. Her right foot is stitched where her small toe was removed, and she has a small scar inside her mouth from the jaw surgery that they performed on her. The cuts on her face and the bruises on her arms have been treated, but they will take a while to heal. She's also in new, comfortable, clean clothes.

Medics from *Destiny's* crew put Alice on a stretcher and then transfer her to one of the medical rooms.

Bogdan, Victor, and Vera stand outside and look at each other without saying anything.

"Maybe now you can tell us," she says to Victor.

He frowns at her, confused. "What?"

"Where was it? Where did Luigi hide the files?"

Victor laughs. "Leo . . . my dog. The last gift from Grandpa. When Leo had surgery, the doctor found it under his skin. I didn't know what it was at first, but I kept it in case it was important. Turned out it was." He pauses for a moment. "Grandpa told me once, 'If you ever feel scared or lonely, just cuddle Leo here on the back of his neck, like this. He has all the answers and will make you feel safe. He's your best friend.' I guess I didn't get the message about the hidden files in his neck, but destiny wanted me to have it." He looks into the distance at the wide blue ocean.

"Well, he was right not to tell you about it. We were always listening. If he told you where the files were, we had microphones all over your house. I actually remember him telling you those things about your dog. Pretty smart move, I must admit. Well, now it's over. Everybody has what they want."

"Not everybody," Bogdan says, lowering his eyes.

Victor and Vera look at Bogdan in confusion seeing as Bogdan has never mentioned anything before.

CHAPTER 62

Great Speech, Mr. Lia(M)R

Liam is in his house in Paris preparing to go to bed. Tomorrow is a big day for him. The French government has decided that Liam is worthy of the Medal of Honor for arresting Alice, who assassinated the French president. He's a hero to many people in France, and tomorrow he will give an amazing speech, so everyone will remember him for a long time. Liam is practicing his speech in front of the bathroom mirror.

"Thank you, thank you all very much!" He pauses, imagining fifty thousand people applauding and screaming his name. "It wasn't easy, I'll say that. All those late nights in my office, trying to solve many cases and catch many bad people, all leading to this moment. It all paid off! Never give up, people!" He pauses again because he expects a big round of applause after that statement.

"Alice Hill is obviously one of the biggest criminals ever, taking our dear President Caron's life and on such a holy night. It's proof that we were dealing with a cold-blooded killer who did not have a touch of the emotions in her. I couldn't bring President Caron back to life, but at least as a policeman, as a French citizen, I could at least bring that murderer to justice!" He nods a few times, appreciating all the imaginary applause.

"However, this isn't the end. I will work day and night to find the person who ordered this horrific crime and give him or her the same justice that we gave to Alice Hill. The death penalty! The traitors against humanity deserve nothing less than what they gave to our beloved president!"

Liam crouches to pick up a toothbrush from the bottom drawer, again imagining the applause, when he hears real applause behind him, but it's only a few claps from a single pair of hands.

"And what do you deserve?" a voice asks.

Liam straightens up slowly and looks in the mirror. Emilio is standing a few meters behind him.

"I know you," Liam says. "Wait . . . you're the guy who tried to kill me at the police station a few months ago!" His eyes open wide.

"If I had finished the job, then some of these things would never have happened." Emilio blames himself, but now he's here to correct his mistake.

"Oh, came back to finish the job, I see." Liam looks around slowly to see if there's anything he can use as a weapon. His gun is next to his bed in the bedroom.

"Don't try anything stupid, or it'll be the last thing you do," Emilio says, noting Liam's darting eyes.

"So, is there anything I can say to change your mind?" Liam asks. He knows this guy is no joke. Liam is scared, but he tries not to show it.

"It isn't my choice," Emilio says. "But I have different orders this time. My boss wants a video of you admitting what you did to Alice and that you were aware ahead of time that the president would be assassinated but did nothing to prevent it. Instead you even helped place Alice on that TV crew, so later you could catch her and be a hero."

"Oh . . ." He thinks of his heroic speech that's still officially going to give the following day. "I'm not sure I can do that."

"The video is just insurance for my bosses that you'll stop digging on this case. If you don't, we'll release it publicly."

Liam still has his back turned toward Emilio, speaking to him through the mirror.

"That's all?" Liam asks, confused.

Emilio nods. "That's all. I take a video of you admitting the things I asked, and I leave. Tomorrow, you give a speech, get a medal, and be a hero. My boss doesn't care, as long as you stop digging."

"Give me a second to think about it," Liam says. He's confused. It would be way easier for Emilio to kill him right now, but it kind of makes sense, and until two minutes ago, he thought this was his last moment. Now he has chance to live. "Fuck it," he says. "I'll do it."

Emilio steps back, pulls out his phone, and asks Liam to face him before he starts filming. "OK, go," Emilio says. "Make it short and sweet." He starts recording.

"Um, I'm Lieutenant Liam Mercier, and I'm making this video to say that . . . I was informed that President Caron would be killed a week in advance, and I did nothing to prevent that. Instead I decided to help Alice Hill by arranging for her to be part of the New Year's Eve TV crew, so she could have access to him and poison him." He stops for a moment and exhales, as if he's just realized what he did. "So

I could catch her later and take all the credit for it . . . to be a hero."

Emilio stops recording while Liam looks at the floor, as if he feels ashamed.

"See? That was easy," Emilio says, then fires two bullets into Liam's stomach with a silenced pistol. "Tomorrow, instead of you showing up on stage and being a false hero, we will share this video for the entire world to see who you really are.

Liam falls to the floor, clutching his stomach. "But I . . . you said . . ." The blood from his stomach is crawling all over the bathroom floor while he puts pressure on the bullet holes to slow down the bleeding.

"You will die in this bathroom, and you'll forever be remembered as the biggest traitor that your country and this world has ever seen."

"You lied to me," Liam says, tears running from his eyes.

Emilio shrugs. "Now you know how it feels."

That's the last words Liam hears before he dies in the bathroom of his house, just like Emilio said he would.

Emilio could have easily killed him right away, but then Liam would have died a national hero. Connor wants Liam to be remembered as a traitor, which will also close all the open cases that Liam was investigating about The Nobodies because nobody will believe his research is valid.

CHAPTER 63

The Orders

"What do you mean it's not finished?" Vera asks.

"Are we just going to let that guy Emilio walk? He betrayed and poisoned Luigi. He killed my father, Victor's grandfather, and your . . . well . . . I'm not sure what he was to you."

"Victor, can you give us some privacy, please?" Vera asks. "Go and check on your 'friend.'"

Victor realizes she wants to talk about something serious with Bogdan, her son, so he leaves, knowing Bogdan will tell him later anyway.

"Listen, my son, as much as I don't want admit it, he was just following orders."

"Then, let's—"

"What? Kill the guy who gave him the order? Is that what you're saying?" she asks, her smile mirroring the sarcasm in her voice.

Bogdan looks at her. He knows it's an impossible mission.

"I will tell you, from my heart . . ." She approaches and takes his hands. "Your father was a very passionate man, a fighter, very stubborn, and very hardheaded. He was a good person, but I warned him not to turn his back on the committee and that we would find another way. He didn't listen, even though he knew the consequences. And honestly, it's just happened to be Emilio. Connor could have asked me to do it, and I would have had no choice." She looks away.

"There's always a choice," Bogdan says quietly.

"Yes, there is," Vera says. "What would you have chosen? To give up on the man who was so hardheaded that he got himself killed and never see you again, my son? By trying to help your stubborn father, I would have gotten you, me, and your father killed. I know I had a choice, and I made one. Now your father is alive through you. And look, his stubbornness is still there."

Bogdan chuckles softly.

"Speaking of Emilio, remember what I told you the first day when we spoke? He saved my life in that house when Pierre and Gamba tried to poison me. At that time, Emilio was also following Connor's orders. Without that, without these two guys taking action, you and me would not be having this conversation right now, and you'd probably have spent your entire life without knowing who your parents were."

Bogdan looks at her. He knows it will take time to accept that she's actually his mother, but for the moment, he likes it when she's at his side.

CHAPTER 64

Am I In Heaven?

Alice slowly opens her eyes and sees a few people around her, but her vision is foggy, and she can't tell who they are.

Victor asks all the medical crew to leave the room for a few moments to give them some space.

Alice notices there is now only one person in front of her. Is it Douglas Routley? She starts feeling the same fear, thinking she's still in that "chair of pain" and expects to be punched at any moment. She tries to lift her hands to defend her face, and surprisingly, she succeeds. Her hands aren't secured anymore.

Alice sits up and realizes she's sitting on a medical bed. She looks in front of her and sees . . . Victor?

She can't help it; she starts laughing like she's on mushrooms. "Oohh, this is so amazing. Hey, Douglas Routley, which drugs did you give me to create these awesome hallucinations?"

Victor is a bit confused but is aware of the state of Alice's mind after everything she has been through. "It isn't a hallucination," he says, speaking slowly and clearly. "It's real."

"Oh, come on, man! What would Victor be doing in this room with Douglas and me?" She continues to laugh.

"Listen, Alice, I don't know who Douglas Routley is, but you're safe now. You're not in prison anymore. The Nobodies saved you."

"Wait." Alice looks down at her right foot and sees a bandage where her small toe used to be. She touches herself everywhere, going over her bruises and cuts with her hands. "Mirror . . . A mirror, please."

Victor finds a small mirror on the table next to them and turns it to face her. Alice looks at herself for a few moments and then takes the mirror from his hand and puts it on her bed.

"So it's really you, Victor?" She starts believing, slowly and carefully, because she doesn't want to be disappointed if this is just a dream or a hallucination.

"Yes, it's me," Victor says calmly.

"But why are you here? Where's your wife?" She's still disoriented and confused.

Victor chuckles for a moment at the irony. "We're not together anymore."

"Oh. OK." Her face doesn't change.

Victor notices Alice is pinching herself on the arm. "Alice, this is all real. Try to relax. You're completely safe here."

"But how did you . . . Who saved me? Where's Douglas Routley?" She looks around in confusion.

"I . . . I don't know who that is, Alice."

"The guy who . . ." She lifts her right foot, showing him where her toe is missing.

Victor realizes Douglas Routley is the person who did these things to her. "He isn't on this boat. Don't worry."

Alice jumps. "We're on a boat?"

"Um, yes, we are, why?"

"Is it safe outside?"

"Yes, very safe," he says confidently.

"Could you take me outside? I want to see the ocean."

She sounds a bit crazy, but who would not want to see the ocean?

Victor lifts her in his arms and takes her to the front of the yacht. He puts her down, and she leans on the railing. She can feel the wind again, cuddling every inch of her body. She smells the salty water, feels the warm sun on her face.

Alice still can't tell for sure if this is all real or what Victor is doing there and what the hell is going on in general, but after all she's been through, it would be a crime not to enjoy the moment.

She raises her arms like Kate Winslet in *Titanic* and smiles as tears of joy slide down her cheeks and neck. Then she turns around and asks Victor the same thing that he asked her when she saved him from drowning five years earlier. "Am I in heaven?"

Then her lips stretch into the most beautiful smile in the world.

CHAPTER 65

Douglas Routley

Seven days earlier

Douglas Routley is sent by someone at the top of the American intelligence network to do anything it takes to get every bit of information from Alice Hill that can be used to determine who assassinated the American president. It's part of a secret agreement with the French government, completely off the books. No one else knows about it, and its completely illegal. Even in prison people still have human rights. However, as soon as Alice was arrested, even before the trial started, it was decided that she would be sentenced to death by lethal injection.

It's easy. Alice doesn't have anyone to back her up. She doesn't want a lawyer, and no one is asking about her health. She's truly a nobody.

Douglas Routley has simple instructions: "Do as you please, but come back with valuable information before she's executed." He has the email address of just one person from the American government, and he's instructed to send a coded email at the end of each day to let them know if he discovers any new information.

On the first night of his arrival, the day before Alice's trial, Routley arrives at a motel near the prison, dragging his big black wheeled case. He needs to stay in a low-profile motel; he's not even in France officially, but he's a bit upset that the garbage bins in his room are still full from the previous guest.

A few minutes after he gets comfortable in his room, someone knocks on his door.

"Housekeeping!"

Routley stands up and opens the door, revealing a guy with a housekeeping trolley.

"Excuse me, sir," the man says. "We forgot to empty your garbage bins. It will just take me a few seconds."

"Sure, come in," Routley says, relieved that they remembered.

The moment he turns his back to the "housekeeper," he feels a strong pain in the back of the head just before he falls to the floor, blood running out of a bullet hole in the back of his head.

That's the moment when Nicos Samaras, the "housekeeper" and a master of disguise, assumes Douglas Routley's identity.

Nicos uses the housekeeping trolley to clean the room and then transport Routley to his car and dispose the body in the nearby ocean.

It's a routine job for a guy like Nicos to prepare himself in makeup, including the long grey hair and beard that are Routley's trademarks.

Connor's reliable hacker "N/A," as usual, provided detailed information to Connor on Routley's behavior and duties, and Connor sent the plan to Nicos, who accepted the mission, which was marked as optional.

Nicos knows that for the plan to work, he only has one try, as always. He needs to be very convincing in the eyes of the prison warden and security guards who observe him while he "works."

Connor orders Nicos to try to get any information from Alice about The Nobodies, and only if she's not a threat is he allowed to rescue her.

Alice suffered terribly with all the punches, cuts, broken jaw, and losing her small toe. It was a perfect detail for the security guard to have no doubt in his mind that the other woman's body is actually Alice.

Alice will never know that it was Nicos, a.k.a. Douglas Routley, her torturer, the devil itself, who pulled her out of hell and gave her another chance to live.

Douglas Routley will always be with her. He will always be her biggest fear, her biggest pain, a reminder of the hell on earth that she has been through. Every time she looks at her missing toe, as he promised when they met, two words will echo in her mind . . .

"Douglas Routley."

CHAPTER 66

A Hero Is A Villain, And A Villain Is A Hero

WNC is releasing their latest news updates and follow-ups, and the people's favorite, Natalie Archer, is announcing it all live. As always, WNC is the first to get this information.

"Alice Hill has escaped from prison! We should have more information soon, but it looks like someone from the outside helped her. This escape means the world's governments and their organizations haven't made any progress in finding the assassins. They are even going backward now, letting someone this valuable slip through their fingers.

"On another note, the 'Hero of France' has turned out to be the 'Traitor of France,' as you'll see in this exclusive video."

The video of Liam admitting everything goes live, and the entire world sees his true face.

"If we can't trust our lieutenants, detectives, and policemen, whom we trust?" Natalie asks. "If the policemen and the governments are villains, does that mean this 'villain' who is fighting them is actually a hero?"

Natalie turns a few pages in a book in front of her. "Let's sum up a few things. Over two thousand poachers were killed in Zimbabwe just a few months ago. The Meng Virus has killed over one hundred and eighty thousand people between China and India. The Angel Mosquitos have now brought death to thirty-six thousand people around the world. Multiple world leaders were killed on New Year's Eve, and Alice Hill, the only assassin captured, has now escaped. Who is this mysterious person who, at the moment, controls the world? Whoever planned and organized all of this has no equal, wouldn't you agree? The only question is, what's next?" She holds on to that question as she closes the notebook in front of her.

CHAPTER 67

The Oranges

Connor turns the TV off after watching the news, stands up, and breaths in and out. Natalie's words echo in his head, "What's next?"

He knows the answer to that question. Nothing. There are no new projects. The Meng Virus and the Angel Mosquitos are still out there, and he is waiting on the world's governments to make a move in disarming their nuclear weapons. He isn't planning any other assassinations at the moment.

Connor puts on a jacket and goes for a walk to his favorite grocery store. It's dark already, just a few minutes before 10:00 p.m. He does not see many people outside; it's very cold. He looks at the sky. It's clear, the stars are shining brightly, and he enjoys the moment.

Suddenly, he starts thinking about everything, about all the years behind him, all the people, dead and alive. A man like him has so many thoughts stuck in the drawers of his brain. As soon as he opens one, the others start opening themselves.

He knows the store will close at 10:00 p.m., so he banishes those thoughts and rushes to the store.

Julia is just closing when he gets there. He turns back, not wanting her to reopen just for him.

"Hey, Mr. Jones!" Julia says. "Did you want something from the store?"

"No, no it's nothing essential," Connor says. "I just wanted to buy some oranges, but it can wait till morning."

Julia smiles. "Don't be silly. Wait here. I'll grab some, on the house!" She goes to unlock the door.

"No, I don't want you to get in trouble." He motions for her to stop.

"OK, you can pay tomorrow. My gosh, it's just oranges." She goes inside and puts six oranges into a bag, then returns to him. "Here you go! Is that enough?"

Connor smiles. "More than enough. Thank you, Julia. I'll come by tomorrow to pay. I don't have any cash, just a credit card. Are you here in the morning?"

"Yes, stupid back-to-back shifts, but it's OK; I get the afternoon off." She goes to lock the store again.

"Well, try to get some sleep," Connor says. "See you tomorrow. Thanks again." He raises the bag of oranges and points it at her.

"Maybe you can do me a favor," Julia says. "I mean, if you're not too busy."

"Sure, what is it?"

"Could you walk me to the bus station? Keep me company on this cold night?"

The bus station is nearby. Connor knows Julia likes him, but he doesn't want to become close with her. He isn't close with anyone, but he feels that this is a simple, innocent thing, just a little thank-you for the oranges and for her being a good human being.

"I can do that," Connor says, thinking there's no harm in it. Or maybe he just wants to spend more time with her, so he finds an excuse for himself.

"So, what do you think about these crazy things happening around the world?" Julia asks as they walk.

"Crazy things?" He looks at her, confused.

"You know, all these presidential assassinations, viruses, mosquitos? It's just February, and so many things are happening already."

"I mean . . ." Of all people, how can *he* properly answer that question?

Julia eyes him curiously. "You don't think the world is a mess right now?"

Connor shrugs. "Sure. A lot of things are happening right now." He tries to shake off the topic.

"We're lucky we're in Switzerland," Julia says. "But I mean, the governments of those countries with nuclear weapons aren't doing shit, and people keep dying." She sounds a bit angry.

"It's a very expensive thing to do," Connor says.

"But not as expensive as people's lives, is it?" She stops and looks at him seriously.

Connor is surprised. He looks at Julia and sees hope. There are more people out there who care about things other than money. "You're right," he says, nodding. "I can't argue with that."

"I don't even think the guy who's doing this is bad at all because if you think about it, it's all kind of necessary," she says with confidence in her voice.

"Why do you think it's a guy?" Connor asks.

Julia scoffs. "Oh, come on, it has to be a guy! If it were a lady, she would gossip about it with someone and would be caught the next day. It's a guy. Smart, silent, a bit cruel, but a good person in general and maybe even good looking." She looks at him. "Someone like you, Mr. Jones. Wait, are you the guy?" She stops and looks at him directly in the eyes

Connor is unprepared for this conversation. She looks at him seriously and then starts laughing at Connor's serious face.

"I'm sorry, but you can't be the guy. You're such a good person. You don't have that cruelty inside you." She puts her hand on his shoulder.

"Well, here's the bus station," Connor says, changing the subject while her hand slides off his shoulder.

"Thank you Mr. Jones!" She puts on her earphones and starts playing music so loudly that even Connor can hear it. She starts walking to the bus station, just a few meters away.

Connor sees the bus coming. He turns around and begins to walk but then turns around again.

The bus is going too fast. He looks at the traffic light and notices that it's yellow. He realizes the driver is trying to catch the light.

Connor looks at the asphalt. It's icy in certain places. It was raining that morning. He realizes the driver won't be able to stop.

"Julia!" he yells, but she can't hear him over her music, and she's looking at her cellphone.

"Damn it!" Connor runs toward her as the bus driver starts braking and loses control of the huge vehicle.

The bus starts rotating, and at the last moment Connor grabs Julia's hoodie and pulls her back before the rear end of the bus hits her.

There is not enough time for Connor to get out of the way though, and the rear end of the bus hits him so hard that he flies through the glass bus stop before hitting a stainless-steel pipe with his head and falling to the ground amidst a shower of broken glass.

CHAPTER 68

The Day When God Became A Human

One day after the accident

Vera walks into the hospital room together with one of the doctors in charge of Connor's case.

Connor's accident is a big thing even without the world knowing who he really is because in Bern, Switzerland, such accidents are rare, so it makes the front page of the newspapers.

"The surgery was nearly six hours, and he did well," the doctor says. "Unfortunately, the biggest damage is inside his head. We removed hundreds of pieces of glass from his skin, body, and head. It was everywhere. He was very unlucky to hit his head on the stainless-steel pipe of the bus stop, which caused him more damage than the glass. He's in a coma right now and, sadly, we can't say how long that will last. It could be days. It could be years. For him, waking up from this coma will be equal to a miracle, but even if he eventually wakes up, he will have lifelong problems caused by the severe damage to his head. Memory loss, hallucinations, we're still not sure if he will be able to walk again or hear properly. He might even wake up completely blind."

"Thank you, doctor," Vera says. "I'll cover all the expenses. He's my best friend, and we've known each other for our entire lives. Whatever it costs and whatever it takes to keep him in a coma but alive and hoping for a miracle, please do it. If you have any questions, this is my number. He doesn't have any family, so please contact me with any questions you have."

The doctor thanks Vera and then leaves the room to give her some space.

Vera looks at Connor, lying there without moving, with all the equipment and needles in his body to keep him alive. She has a hard time believing this is actually happening.

For Vera, Connor is the meaning of untouchable, indestructible, pure power, the Human God, as she called him once. But now he looks so vulnerable and weak. It's weird, but for the first time, he looks like "just a human" in her eyes.

Has karma finally got its hands on Connor? He isn't a saint; that's clear. What more, he's probably the human who has caused the most deaths ever, and it's still happening with the Meng Virus and the Angel Mosquitos, even with him lying there.

Bad people are dying—she needs to give him that—the worst people were always his targets in everything he did. He believed he was working for the greater good, and most of the things actually needed to be done, but no one was willing to be cruel and kind at the same time to get the things done.

In the end, he put himself in this situation by saving someone else's life, not when he was taking all those lives.

How can someone appreciate life to the point that he's willing to give his life for someone else and, at the same time, kill hundreds of thousands of people? Connor is an enigma above all things.

Her heart breaks to see him like this, but this is life, its bitter side, and Vera knows crying will not help, even though she does cry inside. It's ripping her chest apart, but she believes if anyone can pull off a miracle, it is the "Human God."

"Are you his wife?" Julia asks. She went down to make herself a coffee, but she has been next to Connor all night.

"What? No, he's my friend," Vera says. "Who are you?" She knows Connor does not have any family.

"He . . . Mr. Jones saved me . . . Last night." She starts crying again. "I'm sorry, I thought I was done crying." She pulls out a tissue and wipes her face and nose.

"Was it like it says in the newspapers?" Vera asks quietly.

Julia shakes her head. "I don't read it. He pulled me. I had my earphones in, and I couldn't hear it. But he couldn't get out of the way in time . . ." She continues explaining as she demonstrates what happened.

"How do you know Connor?" Vera asks. "Are you his girlfriend?" She looks her up and down. She's very young. "His daughter?"

"What? No! Mr. Jones has been a regular in our grocery store for years. Last night he came by, and I asked him if he could walk me to the bus station—you know, just to keep me company—and he did it. I mean, if he hadn't, maybe . . . I don't know . . ." She scratches her head.

"You didn't know, so don't be too hard on yourself." She's surprised that Connor agreed to keep her company. She's beautiful but very young. Knowing Connor, it sounds like the first time he ever dropped his guard and acted like a human. And then this happened.

They hear footsteps behind them. Vera recognizes the person approaching. Emilio . . .

"How is he?" he asks, entering the room.

"He's in a coma, and the doctors don't know if he's ever going to wake up. It might take years." Vera thinks it's weird that he's there.

"Is he in pain?" he asks, his tone cold.

Vera is a bit suspicious about this question. Knowing Emilio, he might pull the plug out and "help" Connor go to the "better place" to save him from pain and misery.

"No, no pain," she says. She actually has no idea.

"Come out with me," he says, gesturing to Vera. He notices Julia is watching, so he tries not to look suspicious. "Just for a moment."

They go out in front of the hospital. "Connor and I talked about many bad scenarios and what I should do if anything ever happens to him, and he told me that if a scenario like this ever occurred, I should pull the plug." He looks at her without blinking, his eyes half-closed.

"That isn't happening," Vera says. She knows it might be true. Connor would not like to be seen as vulnerable like this by anyone.

"I agree. I don't want to do it," Emilio says quickly. Vera looks at him in surprise. "I believe he can get better," Emilio continues.

"Thank you," she says. I believe it too." She's relieved at his words.

"I'm done," Emilio announces.

Vera frowns in confusion. "Done?"

"Connor's brilliance was the main reason for me to be part of the Nobodies team—no offense. I know you'll take care of him. I guess if he ever wakes up, I'll come by to say hello, but if that never happens, this is the last time you'll be seeing me." He turns and starts walking slowly.

"May I ask just one question?" Vera says, her eyes narrowing.

He stops without turning around. Vera looks around. No one else is within earshot. "Do you ever feel sorry for what you did to Luigi?"

Emilio is silent for a few seconds. She doesn't breathe as she waits for the answer.

"Do you ever feel sorry that you never did anything to stop me?" He says as he walks away.

CHAPTER 69

Connor's World

Five years later

The world is slowly returning to a "new normal."

Over two billion people have died from the Meng Virus—a little over a billion in China and the same in India. A vaccine was developed a few months ago, and now most people have been vaccinated.

However, China and India have suffered unprecedented losses and dropped their population from 1.5 billion people each to 400 million each. It's a horror story that has already being written in the new, updated versions of school history books around the world.

However, as the impact of the Meng Virus diminishes, especially for these two countries, everything starts settling back into place, piece by piece.

There's way more food for everyone, and hardly anyone has died from starvation over the past two years, which was one of the biggest problems in these two overpopulated countries. The employment situation is similar. There's enough work for everyone now.

The Angel Mosquitos, however, are still a mystery, and a cure or vaccine for them has not been found. The Angel Mosquitos have wiped out another 2.5 billion people around the globe. They are regarded as the biggest killer in the history of humanity.

The companies that in the past made billions of dollars selling cigarettes, alcohol, and drugs have gone bankrupt, and their factories are closed because no one is buying those products anymore.

Considering all the people who have died around the world, it took time, but people are finally aware that with the Angel Mosquitos, they have a simple choice: avoid cigarettes, drugs, and alcohol, and they'll be just fine.

Well, except for those unfortunate carriers of deadly transmittable diseases. In that case, there isn't much that people can do. Such people can still live sealed inside their homes, so the deadly disease that they're carrying won't spread any further.

The natural world has recovered completely. The Poachers Massacre in Zimbabwe five years earlier convinced everyone that it's better to choose some other sport.

With fewer people comes less pollution, fewer cars, and less smog. With only four billion people on the planet, less food is required, which means the natural world is reborn.

Best of all, diseases like tuberculosis, AIDS, Zika, malaria, and pneumonia are on the brick of extinction. It's cruel, but the Angel Mosquitos have wiped out over 90 percent of the people carrying these diseases.

Oh, and yeah, the regular, useless, mosquitos are extinct.

This is a new chapter in human history, a new world with more food, more jobs, less pollution, almost no sick people, no alcohol, drugs, or cigarettes, and with a beautiful natural world, which people now treat with respect.

And no longer on the brink of the nuclear war it faced five years earlier. With all that's happened, the human mentality has changed, and there are fewer bad people, less crime, and less greed. Except with governments, of course. Greed is still alive and well there. Although they never fulfill Connor's request to disarm, they realize that they probably will never use their nuclear weapons anyway, not in this "perfect world."

Connor's world.

CHAPTER 70

What Would You Do?

Five years have passed, and Nala is still enjoying her tea business, her country, her family, nature, and peace of mind. Sometimes she likes to think that what she did for The Nobodies in the past helped create a better world. She certainly played her part.

Klaus never gets tired of flying his plane—or better to say planes—because he has a few, and he has even named them all. His favorite is a light-blue Piper Pacer PA-20, which he named *The Nobody.*

Branimir got married, and he and his wife love their life on the farm. They are busy every day with many domestic animals and many nice fields away from the city. It's perfect.

Recently, they had a daughter. Although Branimir will never forget the daughter who was killed during America's bombing of Serbia, he decides to let her rest in peace and knows she will be happy to see that he has managed to move on after a long time.

Tao Woo passed away two years ago at age eighty-seven. Two years before that, he was informed by N/A, Connor's main hacker, about Connor being in a coma with no hopes of waking up, so Tao Woo decided to close his laboratory and spend some time with his family because he feels he has grown old in this lab, and he doesn't have much time left.

Bogdan bought a place next to Victor and Alice's house. He had to because D needed to take care of an old boy Leo. They are inseparable, so he needs to stay close.

D is still full of energy but Leo isn't much of an athlete anymore. He prefers cuddling with D and lying in the shade.

This world is different. Bogdan thinks that every day while kicking the ball in his yard. He misses playing football, but hasn't been able to do it for a long time because when he does, he feels a strong pain under those two bullet scars that he "earned" on the Isle Of Man that night.

Seeing or touching those scars reminds him that he isn't a bad man, and he never was no matter what he did in the past. It was his destiny to do it. He was removing bad people from the planet, and he's proud that, in a small way, he helped build this new era.

Nicos decided that after what he did to Alice, it was time to get out of that "business." He knows he saved her life and helped her, but even now, five years later, he still dreams about her sitting on that chair covered in blood, bruises, and cuts caused by his own hands.

Nicos wants to find Alice. He doesn't want to get credit or a thank-you from her. He's not bothered that she doesn't know who saved her life. He just wants to say he's sorry. However, he has never managed to find any information on her. Nicos knows, that's a good thing. She's probably living under a different name and has a different appearance.

It's New Year's Eve, five years after that famous New Year's Eve. Nicos is dressed as Santa Clause somewhere in Athens, Greece. This time, there are no guns, bombs, knives, or any other weapons under his costume.

But there are a lot of candies and small gifts under the costume that Nicos plans to give to the kids that he meets while walking the shiny, decorated streets of Athens on that beautiful night.

He's the best Santa. He's doing it because it makes him happy to see the kids' reactions and smiles.

He's using his costumes, masks, and acting talent in a different way now but with the same purpose: to make "some people" happy . . .

Victor and Alice have been together now for five years. They didn't bother getting married because they know that the fewer public activities that Alice participates in, the better.

The manhunt has stalled a bit after five years. The authorities are still looking for her, but the investigation has slowed down.

Victor, Alice, and Bogdan are sitting in their fenced yard on the small playground what used to be Lucy's garden and talking while little Luigi, Victor and Alice's three-year-old son, plays with his toys in front of them on a blue blanket surrounded by freshly cut grass.

Victor chuckles. "What is it?" Alice asks, looking at him.

"I was just thinking. At one point, I couldn't tell for sure if I would see tomorrow morning because I had so many problems with The Nobodies and everything, and now I'm sitting here with you and little Luigi many years later and having the most fantastic life ever. I just don't understand. We're the bad guys. If life were a movie, we would be caught in the end." He looks at the grass in front of them.

"Well, I was five days away from a lethal injection," Alice says. "I was sure that was my end, the end of a bad girl." She joins him in staring at the grass.

"Maybe we've paid our debts with our suffering already," Bogdan says. He sneaks up behind little Luigi and lifts him high in the air. "We all suffered; I'll give you that."

"But it's crazy to think that four billion people are gone, just like that." She snaps her fingers. She looks at Victor. "If you were in Connor's place, and you had all that money and power, would you have done the same?"

Victor shakes his head slowly. "No. I don't think anybody would do something like that. His acts were, I know it sounds weird, but apart from the fact they were cruel, they were also kind of . . . not selfish . . . It looked like his whole life, he played God, and from all those stories from Vera, I can't remember that even once he wanted something for himself. Fame, more money, to conquer something. It's weird. It's like his entire life he didn't think of himself, only about other people's lives." Connor is an enigma for all of them but especially for Victor, who has thought about him often.

Vera told them a lot about Connor after he spent a few years in a coma. She wants his legend to live. They know about the accident and that he's been in a coma for five years now, though Vera has never told them where he's being held.

"Not just people," Alice says. "Remember the Poachers Massacre? He thought of animals' lives as well."

"And still, he never got caught." Victor rubs his chin with his thumb and index finger. "Not by governments anyway. He was finally caught by destiny itself."

They fall silent for a moment.

"You guys think he's ever gonna wake up from the coma?" Alice asks.

"Vera says the doctors have lost all hope," Bogdan says. "Technology is the only thing keeping his heart beating."

Victor chuckles again. "What?" Bogdan asks.

"I just thought for a second . . . a guy like this . . . I would not be surprised if he makes a deal with God for one more chance." He smiles.

"Or the devil," Alice says. "You never know; this guy has connections everywhere."

They all have a good laugh . . .

"You would think if that happened, he would search for us, now that we know a lot about him." Bogdan glances at Victor and Alice.

They look at him seriously.

"I hope we never find out," Victor says.

CHAPTER 71

"It's Santa!"

Luca Rosso opens a bottle of champagne in his house in Pisa, Italy. He has two daughters now and is married to a beautiful Italian brunette, Maria Gotti.

Luca couldn't be happier. His daughters, Lola and Selena, are now two and three years old, respectively, and they don't know anything about Luca's past. Neither does Maria.

It's New Year's Eve, and they are together waiting for the year 2025. Luca can't believe how fast time goes. Every New Year's Eve, he thinks of how old Ming, the son of the North Korean leader that Luca assassinated, is now. The same is true this New Year's Eve.

Wow, he's fifteen years old now, Luca thinks. He always hopes that Ming will forgive him and that he's doing well now, but those eyes, that look that Ming had, will be with Luca forever. Luca knew that instantly five years ago, and he was right; he's never been able to forget it.

Luca shakes off the memories and pours champagne for him and Maria and a non-alcoholic kids' version of champagne for Lola and Selena.

They sit in front of the TV, enjoying a New Year's Eve program. The girls love it. Then the doorbell rings.

"It's Santa!" Selena says. The whole family has a good laugh.

"OK, I'll go greet 'Santa,'" Luca says. "You girls better be ready. It's New Year's in a few minutes!" He quickly finishes his champagne, then leaves the glass on the table and rushes to the door because he doesn't want to miss the countdown.

He opens the door and sees a man dressed in black with a black ski mask that covers everything but his eyes.

Those eyes. Luca gets an instant flashback.

It's Ming.

Ming doesn't say a word, just fires two bullets—one in the jaw and another in the forehead, the same way Luca killed his father five years earlier.

In front of his family.

On New Year's Eve . . .

CHAPTER 72

The Biggest Secret

Connor never mentioned to any of his partners or friends—not even Gamba, Pierre, or Vera—how, in recent years, he always had all the information first, even before them, because when they started out, they were all on the same level. They all had their Ears and Eyes, people who acted as informants all over the world, but it was like he had better informants than them.

Connor's ability to get the information first made him more dangerous and the unofficial leader of the group. Vera, Gamba, and Pierre never asked, and for them, it remained a mystery.

N/A, which stands for "Not Applicable" or "Not Available," is the name of Connor's strongest asset, his most secret employee, the best hacker in the world by far. With Connor being in a coma for five years and The Nobodies having finished, Connor's partnership with N/A is over.

Yet, N/A made a huge difference in Connor's favor. N/A always had answers, locations, details, absolutely any information Connor needed, and N/A was the one who sent the missions and details through the Nobodies app. N/A also created the app.

It remains unknown how the two of them started working together. The most interesting thing is, not even Connor knew who N/A was.

Connor was suspicious in the beginning about sharing and accepting any information from N/A, but as time passed, he began to trust, and sometimes he wondered who was on the other side. Who was N/A? However, he knew it was better for both of them if he never found out.

But still, he couldn't help but think there was one more person in the world who always got the information first, way before anyone else.

The fire, the beauty, the unstoppable woman, the fearless Natalie Archer.

Did "N/A" stand for Natalie Archer?

Connor will never know . . .

That he was right.

CHAPTER 73

Goodbye, Connor

Every New Year's Eve, Vera comes into the hospital and waits until midnight, then spends a few hours next to Connor's bed.

Vera is looking and feeling great. Thanks to the Angel Mosquitos, she stopped drinking five years ago, and it's been very beneficial for her.

But tonight she's especially emotional. Connor has been lying in this bed for five years. Over that time, he's lost weight, his face has gotten skinnier, and it's even hard to see his face properly due to all the breathing equipment that's stuck in his mouth and nose. After a while, even for Vera, it stopped looking like Connor. She knows that the "Human God," as she liked to call him, has become merely a body.

Vera came every day in the beginning, then every week, then every month, then once every few months. She doesn't care any less for him despite how much time has passed. She just realizes that she needs to live her life as well, to spend some time with Bogdan, her son.

Vera has sacrificed her family life for The Nobodies, and now it's time that gets some of that back. Her and Bogdan have become close. He's even started calling her "Mom," and she's very happy about it.

Tonight it's different for Vera. She has decided to pull the plug, to stop the machines that are keeping Connor's body alive. She can't stand to see him anymore in this vegetative state.

Vera made the doctors aware of that earlier in the day, though it's not really the doctors' call.

It's heartbreaking for her. She has thought for many years about doing it, and she has finally decided it's the best thing to do.

There's one more thing . . .

Vera notified Emilio and Julia, as his last friends, to come and say their final goodbyes.

She also invited Bogdan, Victor, and Alice to come and see Connor for the first and last time, because now it no longer makes any difference.

Only Julia responded, saying she would not be able to come because she is in another country celebrating New Year's Eve with her boyfriend, stating that "It's time to start a new life."

It's been a few months since she last saw Connor, but Vera knows Julia isn't bad. For a young girl like that to visit for over four years is a sign of respect.

Vera hears footsteps, and she turns around as Victor, Alice, little Luigi, and Bogdan enter the room. It's around 10:00 p.m., and they don't want to miss the chance to see the man who controlled their lives for so many years, the man who changed the world.

They walk slowly toward Connor's bed.

"Still hard to believe," Alice whispers.

"What's that?" Vera asks, looking at her.

"This man here killed over four billion people. I mean, his actions, his orders. Only one man . . ." She shakes her head.

"But he did make the world a better place," Victor says, "and the world will never know who he is."

"Did you ever think of, like, sending an anonymous letter to some TV channel or something just so he isn't forgotten, so he doesn't die like a—"

"Nobody," Emilio says as he walks in. Everyone looks at him for a moment. "If he could choose, he would die as a nobody. It's never *who* is doing it that's important; it's *what* has been done. The act is more important than the performer. That was his logic."

"This is Emilio," Vera says, introducing him to the others. "I don't want any drama; this night is emotional enough already!" She's very serious as she looks at Victor and Bogdan. She knows Emilio will act like a professional.

Victor and Bogdan have both cooled down from wanting to get revenge on Emilio. They understand that Grandpa Luigi crossed the line, and they decided to leave everything that's in the past stay in the past, so they could move on and have a normal life.

"Don't worry," Victor says. "Everything is fine." He's calm, although a touch of anger flows through his veins. He has left that whole thing with Luigi in the past, but now this man, his grandfather's killer, is standing right in front of him.

"All good," Bogdan says. He never met Luigi, so he feels fine in Emilio's presence. He knows this man saved his mother's life.

Emilio crouches in front of little Luigi. Alice looks at Vera, as if wondering if her son is safe. Victor and Bogdan are on their toes in case he tries something.

"You're Luigi, I assume," Emilio says. He's very close, right in front of the boy's face. "You have the same name as my best friend. You also have his blood. I had a lot of respect for your great-grandfather, the same respect I have for this great guy here." He points at Connor. "Respect is the only thing that matters in this world. Remember that." He pulls a golden Italian necklace out of his pocket. "I've had this with me for so many years. It's kept me safe. It's from your great-grandfather. Here, let's see how it looks on you, handsome." He places it over Luigi's head and around his neck. "Once you're big and strong, you can wear it, and the spirit of your Great-grandfather Luigi will always be there to protect you."

Everyone is silent for a moment. Nobody expected anything like this from Emilio. Everyone is in the verge of tears. Vera finally gets an answer to her question about whether Emilio has ever felt sorry about what he did to Luigi.

Everyone except Alice. She's still expecting something evil from Emilio, as if he might strangle little Luigi with that golden chain. She has only heard bad things about him.

Emilio stands up and turns to Alice. "I want you to know that he cried like a coward at the end."

"Who cried like—" It takes her a moment to realize that Emilio is talking about Liam.

It takes just a blink of an eye for all that fear, all the bad expectations from Emilio's side to go away. He's a different person in her eyes now. She feels . . . gratitude.

"Don't thank me," Emilio says. "It was his idea." He nods toward Connor and then steps back and stands calmly at the far end of the room, near the door. Everyone turns to look at Connor.

"So, you don't think he'll ever wake up?" Alice asks. She's feeling sorry for this ending for Connor. She never know him, but it's almost like she did considering the effect he had on her life.

"At one point, maybe about a year ago, the doctors actually had hope," Vera says, "but they don't anymore, especially with all the time that's passed. I mean, five years . . . The truth is, he's alive because of all this expensive equipment on his face and around him."

"He's an outstanding man," Emilio says. "One in a million. Vera's right; he wouldn't want this. I only wish he could see the world he created." He nods to Vera, indicating that he's ready.

"Do you want to go closer and say goodbye before I—"

Emilio shakes his head. "No, I want to remember his face, him at his best, not like this."

Vera nods in understanding. She will always remember him at his best, no matter what. "OK, my friend," she says, turning to Connor. "Safe travels. You'll always be looking over our shoulders. I know that because that's what you do. You've always been a ghost in this world. The world never saw you, but you saw the whole world, and you changed that world. Until we meet again . . ." With that, she pulls the plug.

Electronic vital sign monitors stop beeping in the pattern of a heartbeat. Soon they emit a long beeping sound, announcing that Connor's heart has stopped.

Emilio leaves the room immediately.

As Vera sits on a chair next to Connor's bed, tears run down her face.

"Let's go," Bogdan whispers to Victor and Alice. "Give her some space."

All four of them leave the room . . .

It's easier for Vera. Before she pulled the plug, she planned that moment for years. She's mentally prepared but not for this. Now that he's really gone, everything feels more real.

Vera stands up and starts removing the medical equipment from Connor's face. She wants to hug her friend and kiss his cheek for the last time before she leaves the room.

Vera stares at Connor as her tears kept running. So many memories . . .

For a moment, she gets serious, wipes her tears, and takes a deep breath, in and out.

She's looking at one spot, like she's thinking . . .

She pulls the blanket that's covering his body higher and covers his face.

Vera's lips start spreading slowly until they form a wide smile. It becomes the widest smile that Vera has ever smiled.

She laughs as she remembers Julia's response when she messaged her to come to say a last goodbye to Connor. She said she was out of the country with her boyfriend, that it was time to start a new chapter in life."

The second part of that message was for Vera. It's a farewell message.

That's the moment, the very second, that Vera realizes that Connor already said goodbye to her, long before they said goodbye to him.

As the dead man lying in bed in front of her isn't Connor at all . . .

How many worlds deep inside ourselves we do not discover because we are too busy in the only world that we have been told is the "real one."

We are all heroes in our own story, and villains in someone else's.

Which superpower would you choose?
Inspiration.

That's not a superpower, what can you do with inspiration?
Anything.

We are who we are, in the world that we did not choose.
Until we discover fiction books.

CPSIA information can be obtained
at www.ICGtesting.com
Printed in the USA
BVHW021923270421
605908BV00005B/34